*johnny werd*

i

# Johnny Werd

# Johnny Werd
## The Fire Continues

### O. Synopsis

Spineless Books  Urbana, Illinois

Johnny Werd: The Fire Continues

by Q. Synopsis

First Spineless Edition published 2003

ISBN (cloth) 0-9724244-1-5  $19.95
ISBN (paper) 0-9724244-2-3  $9.95
formerly published as ISBN 0-7388223-4-5

Spineless Books
Box 515, Urbana, Illinois
61803
USA
spinelessbooks.com

Library of Congress Cataloging-in-Publication Data

Synopsis, Q., 1969-
    Johnny Werd : the fire continues / Q. Synopsis.-- 1st
Spineless ed.
        p. cm.
    ISBN 0-9724244-1-5 (cloth) -- ISBN 0-9724244-2-3
    1. Young men--Fiction. 2. Chemists--Fiction. I. Title.
PS3619.Y58J64 2003
813'.6--dc21
                                        2003000850

# Contents

Johnnywerd is dead ........................................ 5

Part I: "A Tern for the Werse" .......................... 7

Chapter one .................................................. 8

Bukowski's Alimony ........................................ 14

The House house next door ............................... 16

I am everything (cloaked in abstract) .................. 22

Chapter one .................................................. 30

Epilogue ...................................................... 44

Chapter 2 .................................................... 45

Chapter one .................................................. 51

Reflections on being electricity ......................... 51

Epilog ........................................................ 52

Appendix ..................................................... 55

The End ...................................................... 66

Part II ....................................................... 67

The next day ................................................ 68

A couple days later ......................................... 73

Johnny Werd: the truncated .............................. 76

On one of the subsequent days a couple days later ... 79

Two days hence .............................................. 80

Analogous Metamorphosing Technique    84

I smell Johnny Werd    86

Metanoir    91

Temping at Echelon    100

Dow Jones & Union Carbide to Merge    104

Vigi    111

V.    115

Q & A    116

Werkbernout    117

Footnotes    121

*I, werd:*

*wired,*
*weird,*

*begin*
*being*

*this*
*shit.*

*Elvis*
*lives.*

very well then let's start (clears throat) johnny werd as he relates to events in the past present & future (adjusts spectacles) what he does is actually quite simple: using some chemistry equipment and a starter set of elements 1-8 j werd created a serum that would affect human behavior in such a manner that their behavior would er alter but er he had no idea that's what he was doing (glances at notes) because he failed by succeeding when he had anticipated failure he poured the chemical down the drain a symbolic act of defiance

(pauses to project a transparency of the werd *DEFIANCE*

)well the result was dramatic it affected the water and made obvious by the um mail the (takes a drink of water) the concept of control only becomes interesting when we consider the control of the controller. in a system, can one element control, directly or indirectly, all the others without being itself controlled? in the case of the universe presented by Johnny Werd, the president, the controller, is in fact under the control of the system under his control. how? does anybody want to answer that? (taps chalk in palm) well

(writes in large letters on the chalkboard) *POSTCONTROL*

he is controlled retroactively. the mechanisms of rebellion were removed at an early age. his childhood conformed to every other and all his influences were inspected and cleaned by popular appeal. therefore he grew up in a mold. after drinking the water the president only changes in honesty, not in integrity. he was controlled by popular appeal, the soundless and oiled turning of all the gears gleaming. let us examine, for example, his inaugural address:

"is this thing on? despite reports of fire your subservience is not in danger. i'm going golfing: look at my new shoes. my administration is in your homes already. my attempt to appeal to you from a television screen is less false reassurance than a distraction. i smile conversationally while my hands snake into your pockets and gently extract any valuables that might be of use to me and my nation. i am inside your cereal boxes, your faucets and your outlets. we are already convinced that you neither read nor write any article of paper which we did not provide or process.

*johnny werd*

*3*

you do not leave your homes to talk to your neighbors. it is irrefutable: you are watching this speech therefore i am assured that you are sitting on your couch at home and are to be rewarded for your inaction. that is all. please continue watching." (takes another drink of water)

# Johnnywerd is dead

johnnywerd is dead
railroad ties righthroughis head
charcoal brain cussing fluent red

lennt and mcarted the bones in his wake
they felthey had dug a grave mistake
one of them singed while the other one spake

johnny werd is stiffly dead
testubes impale witheir smoothed glass heads
pencils skewer him with #2 lead

johnny werd is mouldering dead
lsd wedged in his head
neon brain quizzing spastic red

johny werd is dead
a dictionary wedged between his head
johnny werd can't play guitar

he never could play guitar

johnny werd was ripped in half
two tried to prevent his drowning
i'm losing my fingers now they're diminishing
I can't type with them for much longer
the keys are getting bigger

clockwork burning
two late in the night
clockwork turning

on stage a man's paper trampled
a thousand mechanical groupies' hearts melted like nuclear slugs
johnny werd walked onstage and was badly mugged

while a thousand record companies dined for his name
ate toast with his shame

and so sat to reminisce that i haven't possibly been like this
in a while

though so sad my large chance was stolen
while groupies oiled the wings
and i was let down
a simple rock and roll bandit pulling another fast one.

# "Good Grief, Johnny Werd!"
## Part I: "A Tern for the Werse"

This is the end of the Entirely Ordinary Story of Johnny Werd.
It is possible that at the end of the story Johnny Werd is insane
and that alone makes this story weird. But I don't think so.

I am not that subtle.

Johnny Werd is last seen upstairs staring into the mirror. The
other side of the mirror is covered with reflections of moths that
do not exist.

Johnny Werd is no longer capable of looking backwards in time,
incapable of answering the question "How did it all happen?"
let alone asking the question
"What happened anyway?"

Gentle reader, please don your asbestos suit.
The story is about to begin.

being an authentic writer is different from being a pretend rock and roll star. the latter is glory without artistry. for example, johnny werd could grasp a gleaming car yellow guitar & ascend the stage in a pyramid of brilliant enlighting. after he figures out where to plug it in then he then experiments with the knobs accidentally stroking the strings with his maroon cuff. not in tune: even stroking unfretted strings produces a weird dischord he hadn't anticipated (having never done it before). he fingers one string uncertainly retreats to pluck another with expert ineptness. another: clash dissonance hum whirlwinds. he shrugs, grimacing meekly at the audience invisible in the glare inaudible in the grind of his wire fumbling abrasive contact pickup & dying whining feedback. eventually the invisible audience cites requests: "freeberd" "ugly nora" "stairway to california" johnny werd never listened to the radio. the only music he has ever enjoyed amounted to Scott Joplin as interpreted by Herb ("Fats") Alpert & the Tijuana Brass on a scratched cylinder of primitive musical code on his grandmother's victrola. he now sits at his desk werking, his redspeckled brow permanently ferrowed like rows of tilled earth fertilized with embryonic ideas. his psyche is a random soup of unstable elements. a plasma of questionmarks: hooks tangled in a sea of dots. johnny werd was not yet experienced with the aging process: the inexplicable & unstoppable acceleration of time in which his tumultuous adolescent anatomy would resolve itselfindulgent process in a theoretical deep baritone throat pulsing veinwebbed musculature & a thick weave of hair radiating from the pubic regions. he had no anticipation of nocternal emission staining the transition from awkward adolescence to the tragedy of fertility: a man whose soul is still geekshaped. ever incapable of getting "some" regardless of the urgent boiling of blood. the record he is listening to through the guestroom wall is Guy Lombardo & the Royal Canadians' Greatest Swing Classics & he whistles merrily along in an unrelated melody free of key. it is late at night & the experiment has been wandering aimlessly for some many hours. Johnny Werd is drunk with fumes of unknown chemicals which froth sinisterly in beakers before him &, accidentally knocking a tube from a burner cascading a fan of toxin across

the tabletop he stands, too exhausted to startle, & in the mirror
an underdeveloped skeleton with oilsaturated pimpleskin &
wild orange hair, thick blackrimmed glasses with a wad of
maskingtape at the bridge stares at him with disgust suspended
in fascination. he is unable to continue treading the gluey waters
of sleepless delirium: overreactionary & impotent. it is past his
bedtime. the junior high morning will too soon sweep across the
horizon triggering clock alarm toxic cattleprod will scrape him
from his mattress the flavor of dream decaying in his mouth to
shovel himself into an idling yellow bus which would lerch &
trundle off to prison. a bizarre existential prison behind whose
bars he is characterized entirely by an underdeveloping body &
uncoolclotheswornimproperly in a circus of carnivaltent mutants
loping gingerly around the sneakertracked gym or being nailed
to involuntarily answer abstract questions in latinclass with a
voice tesseracting octaves or warming the bench at chessteam
scrimmage all sealing selfexile as ostracized geek for some
colorless eternity. he shouldn't have to worry about that here
in his room & solitary confines staring at the boy in the mirror
while acids eat away the artificial wooden desktop in a triangle
of fuming chemical conversion unnoticed. what solution could
johnny werd expect to create from the brand new set of chemicals
contraptions coiled glass & stoppered erlenmeyerflasks, a
rainbow of opaque fluids suspended in glass testubeshaped like
candy bullets. in the milkglass some distilled weirdness rained
drop by drop & a fluctuating mist rose from the pink liquid in
which a gradual & gentle sediment of orange rained down to
collect in the bottom. johnny werd falls asleep with his clothes on
to dream of going to school without them.

the rabid cat, eczematous emphysemic neurotic grey manged
patches of fur marred with white abscessed absences diseased
& wheezing now, is cracking the unlatched door of Jwerd's room
angling the outdated Trustiron Tools calendar's gaudy display
of Miss "U" May wearing only a full belt of ratchet attachments
her long nails marred with axle grease. cat sniffs the sour
chemical aroma daintily with exposed nose quizzical & before
werd opens one eye & flings beaten home ec textbook in its
general direction it neurotically starts & darts under the bed
where it had clawcarved a defensive groove for itself between
querky electric train panorama with working coalmine & plastic
Anatomy Man with the LEDs indicating pressure points &
erogenous zones no longer illuminated by Neveready batteries

defunct & bleeding peanutcolored acids into the grey shag carpet
& oh i don't know the nerfpinballmachine & the whifflegolfball.
actually the cat's fortress is fantastic outrivaling John E. Werd's
most ingenious conceptions of Snoopy's doghouse (7 linesegments
somehow encompassing a chandelier a pool table & one or more
Van Goghs) & even the batcave. the cat nosed aside a ventilating
grid attached with 1 screw & entered a forgotten dumbwaiter.
the dumbwaiter operated automatically by a system of pulleys &
counterweights & cat was just heavy enough (despite a bulimic
inability to hold down kitty chow). the cat suffered, suffering
from a multiplicity of diseases secondly hair tooth & claw loss as
well as severe coughing sneezing fits in adddition to all manner
of misdigestive unpleasantness moreover fleas. & the cat was
traumatized by a buried kitten incident. it had been buried. alive
by the side of a highway in a sack tied to a stone. by another
cat. its mother. on a normal day the cat's slack could be reduced
to as little as Ð% due to these unpleasant treasons. the other
important characters would not be introduced.

let me explain.

on the otherside of the wall downstairs disturbed satyrs stir
silhouetted fluttering against the screened windows of the
kitchen/bathroom/diningroom/livingroom/masterbedroom
where j's parents watch television diligently, the encouched &
balded patriarch draining milkglasses as his heavier half shovels
chocolates. in a civilized trick to avoid discomfort mr.&mrs.werd's
lifestyles never left the sofa. all provisions were within reach,
sink & refrigerated milk & chocolates. mom's left arm is a fleshy
steamshovel maneuvering candies of chocolate across that
unnecessary expanse of air between box & mouth. the box was
heartshaped, provided by the husband father figure dentures
& hairloss sitting watching the president get a manicure. there
was no reason to change the channel. they projected the possible
possibilities in their conversation which was so successful it
had become another channel they never changed. they had
had their conversation thrice. mrs.werd would emphasize the
possibility that the Brady Bunch could function therapeutically
as a catalyst towards the imperceptible process of uniting as a
family. mr.werd would cite "it is probably a rerun" providing an
abrupt bureaucratic halt, a cessation of motivational funding,
& the president would prepare a TVdinner for himself depicted

by three colors interwoven in a digital grid of pixels on the
television screen the president washes his hands & practices his
fifth inaugural address before his bathroom mirror & wonders if
he lost something along the campaign trail. he used to have the
option of bathing in private. now there are always underwater
cameras & lighting equipment, microphones & acoustic tiles. a
bevy of secret service agents continually inspect every corner of
everything. they stripsearched his wife occasionally upon finding
evidence that she had some connection with him. other than all
this, however, it seemed to be an OK job.

weird & wired sealed in the ceiling the lightbulb was screwed.
it had burned in discontent for an eternity & would burn again
for another. if one of the werds was even aware that the brilliant
bulb had berned uninterrupted since the beginning of time &
furthermore for some freak reason decided to do something
(about that needless expenditure of kilowatts) they would first
have to discover the existence of the basement itself, which, due
to a minor architectural oversight had been included underneath
the house with neither entrance nor windows@. the only passage
into the basement did not exist. within the basement there
was neither switch nor fuse in the lightbulb's circuit & it was
far too hot to unscrew using anything short of an asbestos suit
& tongs. the uninterrupted burning without the abrupt ons &
interminable offs of a normal light bulb's existence had caused
this bulb to experience a sort of useless & agonizingly painful
immortality it did not want. however, it remained relatively
marginally sane (for a lightbulb) in the knowledge that any
hypothetical interruption in power would cause its blackened
fracturing filament to disintegrate immediately & mercifully.
in effect the tungsten had dissolved & it was only the searing
passage of electrons that bound the molecules together tragically
because it existed in a fully fictional universe in which the power
poured through the werd's neighborhood & into their home &
into that very sizzling threaded recessed socket in a steady
stream free of irregularities & as a result the lightbulb screamed
continuously in a distant pinwheeling fantasy of decay. each
second lasted much too long & was exactly too painful. oh well,
the lightbulb slowly sizzles into existential nonextinction.

upstairs in the pyramidal rented attic the drooping plant droops
& rotates its thirstwatered fifteenth leaf one second of degree
& this imperceptible twitch may have been almost a thought,
actually a premonition, or only a reflex.

there was another character in the attic, breathing.

in summary, the cat threaded through the plot insignificantly
knocking over the ornate wrought iron ashtray whose stem
rose gracefully three feet over the mr.'s&mrs.'s carpet which
lay invisible in the shadow of the flickering radioactive glow
of television: the ruler masticating green beans & ultimately
driving around in his car his face an expressionless series of
nods as he waved with his left hand at the hungerfed voters who
gazed back uncertainly & the plant.

6:30 & the alarm goes off.

6:31 & now a whispered
werd aside quietly about
johnny while he tosses
in a slow spasm of sleepy
dreams painfully about
the society he did not care
about the society which
shaped him through
authority figureheads
of the society that
addressed him directly
only through magazines:
technical comic tabloid
teen astrology news
pornographic depictions
of the society that
encouraged him to stand
in line at mcdonalds.

6:41 & mildly distracted
by the alarm johnny werd
by default continues to
sleep. the cat wanders
in & out of reality & has
a leukemiatic hacking
fit. from upstairs in
the attic came a erratic
percussive sound & if
johnny werd's perceptions
were so finetuned that
he was able in his sleep
to differentiate & record
the 26 pitches of the
individual clicks he would
be able to decode the
following story...

# Bukowski's Alimony

i didn't expect you. your clarity of
vision you could tell by the utter
shock infiltrating the corners of
my emotionally depleted features
flabby & paralytic in sluggish
inebriation delirium...you had
never seen me so wretched &
unshaven & were not alarmed but
somewhat bemused, coy, distant.
& i surprised & paralyzed like
a woodchuck on the highway
before the light & ascending
pitch of a rapidly advancing
semi-(lennybruce unexpected
of spotlight). & you had never
been so beautiful. & here in this
soiled context, the creases of my
envermined room, cigarettestub
orchestra bottlecultures. goddess
in the elegant drapery of leather
about one shoulder & the girlish
haircut. i prematurely fifty
varicose reeking alcoholic &
bloodshot. i didn't even recognize
you, the mechanics of shock
rusted. your articulately makeup
enhanced features a calendar
following the evolution of fashion
were always too beautiful to be
recognized. i must have stumbled
& spilled bacardi all over
dostoevsky me trying to rescue
the idiot with paralytic fingertips
protesting mostly

"where have you been you
disappeared so abruptly. you
only tried to call me twice" you

breathed fiery. the interchange
was wrong, my communicative
attempts received cruelly like
clumsy jabs from a cold branding
iron my hands only my hands
only hold on hands. you even
waited for me to kiss you. my
weekend weakened heart. you
left me stunned in a corner & i
wanted at once to laugh & collapse
into selfinflicted martyrdom the
tendency being somehow to see my
reflection somehow distorted in
your piercing eyes as you slid out
the door. afterwards i would stare
at my bloodied reflection distorted
in a shard of bottleglass & weep
to myself for my blurred response
mechanisms, my paralysis.
doomed love my expectations
dissolve like a cloud of dispersing
berds...

as the clicking ended mr.werd, realizing his wife was about to
wake up, concealed crime & punishment under the sofa cushion
& began to pretend to continue to watch the president sleep, his
snores translated into seven languages in the lowerhalf of the
screeen. the sofa was orange yellow & brown, sharp plaid. the
carpet was green & blue plaid.

the walls were pink with green polkadots,
some misguided 50's nostalgia.

6:43 where's the cat johnny?
asked his mom in an explosion of
maternal concern blasting wide
the door to his room interrupting
a dreamed subplot involving

Adjusting the glossy pages of her microbiology text with her right hand, Rachel House groped for more strawberries with her left hand, considering the story that lay before her with expectation of afterimage. a premonition occurred.

She felt as though she and her husband Ed were inexplicably linked. their personalities adjacent white blood cells intertwined. an embrace of pseudopods the metaphor in which her and his cell wall textbook diagram symbolism their cell walls conformed and a passage of technical term globules of chemicals passed through their adjacent cell walls from nucleus to nucleus and that therefore her suspicion that Ed, an airline pilot, might be at that very second intertwined with a stewardess in the cramped bathroom of a make of airplane hanging over the glittering Pacific might in fact be justified. her ignorance of the method in which an airplane is flown was grand and complete, like my own.

In this rancid daydream, her dried and sleepless eyes inspected the text, every letter, and not a single word was formed, not a single sentence absorbed, the daydream continued, the information itself the dream, impossible to remember upon wakening. not touched upon in the summary questions at the end of the chapter where she found her eyes had come to rest, awaiting her attention, like leaves floating downstreambound, come aground at a tight bend.

Rachel usually liked dreams. when she had them asleep, that is. not yet cleverly placed paragraphs like this one would indicate that she napped every afternoon when, she found, the likelihood of vivid dream was at its greatest. only in dreaming was she able to fly engaging in sexual intercourse (sometimes with Ed) in midair her wings an effortless passage through all of time and space. discovering only through prolonged dreams the ability to rectify her memories. rewriting her filing cabinet on the seventh hour. therefore her nucleus, peeled upwards, left her cytoplasm and the pseudopodic embrace of Ed.

She realized her vision and attention had wandered away from the glossy text out the window across the peaceful springtime lawn and onto the porch of the somewhat dilipadated Werd house next door. there were two strangers on the porch, men with taut suits and reflective glasses, lean and powerful ties who idled in awkward repose awaiting a response from the doorbell.

*Odd, the Werd's tended not to get visitors. were they from Mr. Werd's company? were they from the electrical company?* she had wondered, realizing that she had no idea what MrorMrs.Werd did for a living. No one answered the door so one of them began to walk around to the back of the house, the other extinguishing his cigarette on the Werd's mailbox. Stranger still, unbuttoning his suit jacket, inserting something into his ear and positioning himself in front of the door. and from Rachel's vantage point she could see a nervous curtain move on the attic window.

The telephone rang and she went to the bedroom to pick it up. It was Ed calling from Linz:

> Ed: hello honey.
>
> Rachel: hello dear.
>
> Ed: just thought i'd call to tell you i'm in swindon. i'll be leaving for Madrid very soon. how are you?
>
> Rachel: i'm fine.
>
> Ed: okay dear. i'm going to hang up now. it was wonderful to talk to you again.
>
> Rachel: you too. miss you.
>
> Ed: miss you too. bye bye.
>
> Rachel: bye bye.

Rachel unwound herself from the telephone cord wondering if Ed had said anything that could possibly negate her suspicion. it was not how she had wanted the conversation to go.

6:43 johnny is awoken. his eyes
reluctantly open. it is morning.
his mickeymouse alarmclock
had failed to awaken him.
mom shoved him from a weird
dream her hand on his pastel
racecarladen pyjamas. she stands
before him silhouetted by the
rising sun visible through the
window its light washing the
entire room.

"is language a status symbol?"
she asks.

"i don't know mom." he replied uncertain whether she had failed
to notice the damage or not or whether she was pretending not to
either to give him a chance to confess exaggerated everything or
to inspire a sense of guilt for the crime he would not be punished
for, the crime of throwing his home ec textbook at the cat causing
it to scuff a sliver of paint off of his bedroom wall. perhaps her
only senses are the auditory and tactile, soles & fingertips, ears.
no tongue in her mouth which kissed his cheek & scolded him. he
would be wearing corderoy today she gently but firmly informed
him.

brown.

behold Johnny's room, in the stellar crystalline swirls of the
sunlit dust settling in the wake of the retreating mom. his
room, on the second level of Werd Estate & Lawn overlooked the
intersection of Domestic & Compliance where the schoolbusline
was forming. friends chad buddha ernie bert & only then louisa
& vanessa were already waiting the boygirl dichotomy existent &
a wall of deliberate miscommunication. the girls had not yet been
taught to conspire against one another in secret alliance with the
oppressive significance of the masculine role. the rising sun was
obscured by the werd place tacky bricktone shingles patchwork &
its rays reached them only through the eastern & subsequently
western windows of Johnny Werd's room, cascading through the
glittering prisms of bottles & beakers, tubes & flasks. colored
chemicals casting inconsistent spectrums. the carpeted roof

(carpeting somehow chemically stable & imperturbable. also the
entire test tube assemblage which was on an exterior corner &
shielded

morningringed & heavy, Johnny chewed through a bowl
of FROOT WHOOPS thoughts meandering as his eyes
rerereread the list of ingredients:

CHARTREUSE #3, $C_8H_{10}N_4O_2$, POISON,
$C_7H_5NO_3S$, $LI_2CO_3$, OPIATED HASHISH,
U 235, PLASTER, WAX, $CH_2O$, WONDER
SIMPLEX 7, WOMBAT FAT, PETROLEUM,
DONUTS, FUSCHIA #3, CHROME PLATING, &
$C_{20}H_{25}N_3O$
TO enhance COLOR!

in this list, W was convinced, lurked the secret to FROOT
WHOOPS! as well as CAP'N WHAM!, MAPLE MANIA!,
even SUGAR CAKED PSYCHEDELIC SEiZIURE-O's! &
PSYCHOCRUNCH!!!. if he could recombine these ingredients he
could create the wonder drug that would affect reality realitors.
their denial mechanism reinhibitors repressed, teachers, (the)
cops (who had prevented him from playing in the swamp), even
adults would become permanent slaves of his every whim. he
had read enough issues of *Religious Tirade Monthly & Overly
Pedantic Literary Reference Index & Technical Jargon Illustrated*
to fully understand everything real & imaginary & otherwise
nonexistent.

except the side of this cereal box..

KIDS OF AMERICA!
GET YOUR COOL
NIRVANA SHADES
AND GAIN
INSTANTANEOUS
ENLIGHTENMENT
FREE ABSOLUTELY
GUARANTEED!!!(by
us) just eat 120
boxes of FROOT
WHOOPS! and
send proof of
digestion and
a million dollars
for shipping
and handling to
TECHNICOLOR
FOOD (simulations)
PO BOX 8456703v1
GRAND RAPIDS
MICHIGAN!
include all
credit cards a
Stradivarius Sitar
Mt. McKinley and
a copy of TWO
HALVES FOR THE
PRICE OF ONE
(LOPE AT THE
HIVE/ONLY THE
STONES REMAIN):
Armageddon EYE1
(1981) by the Soft
Boys total slack the
Hope Diamond
the Lost Continent
of Atlantis and
Eternal Peace.

the cat leapt from the top of the refrigerator did 120 flips then
landed in the cereal bowl splattering wobbling spheres of white
liquid everywhere. Johnny Werd attempted dripping milk from
his orange pipecleaner hair to impale the cat on his fork laced
with tabasco sauce but only sheared off some of its fur. an
escapade occurred in which the television cord was tripped over
causing a short which made the lightbulb downstairs flicker in
a piercing far too near-to-death agony-wrending shriek which
only the cat believed it could hear zigzagging through the dining
room using its manged tail as a propeller. johnny werd pursued
with fork. it is a race to the end. who will win? will johnny werd
prevail as golden trumpeters signal eternity & clouds part &
glorious rays of light lance down impaling cupidlike cherubs who
cavort around the sky until their twin AAA batteries wane &
they fall crashing to earth into tinsel & gilded blue shrapnel of
no use to any of the potential murderers & victims who wander
the park at night when the only light is the eternal funeral flame
commemorating the assassination of the following poem written
by the Late & American Robert Beet. in an ordinary parkbench
feeding pigeons:

# I am everything (cloaked in abstract)

i am the allreferent
obscure hindu term
i am the ultimate
shining god
reference
i am
the
down
trodden
pitiful
i am the
only lone
ignored
existential
martyr
i
am
the
symbolic
artist
poet
i
see
an image
of something
beautiful beyond
tangibility
i am quite
finished
thank
you

after reading this poem in the moving light of the COCACOLA
nostalgia lamp which swung on its chain as three trains passed
over & under & through the house & a right angle pipe in
the corner ceiling opened a mouth & spoke shrieking steam
hissing ambivalent wetdreams of forgotten aztec pyramids &
hotdog vendors lost in the Arabian desert in epic repetition of

repetition of repetition of repetition of repetition of repetition of repetition of repetition of of of repetition of repetition of repetition of repetition of repetition of repetition of repetition of repetition of distorted atonal guitar chords from a nun forgotten hallucination of onstage in which the unamused glares of the audiencemembers was far too real. johnny werd woke up slumped & drowning face in his milkbowl. gasping enough nitrogen to compensate for the decreased oxygen in his suddenly thundering bloodstream johnny werd realized he feels really really invigorated & is ready to cue up at the gallows where the orange jr.highschoolbusdriver would come to hang them all in a sweatshirthooded line: now with additional friends steve spike jason opportunity convenience shed ralph slack jerry ralph pinhead & finally "raisinbr"ed, Johnny B. Werd's best friend. johnny werd arrives last in line fidgeting impatiently because of the mornings dreamed freaking of the cat Johnny Werd is unable to focus his concentration wandered in & out of the focus of the narrative which now has a chance of becoming embogged: entrapped in the eternal mirrored lasergeneration of a single reference to itself. however not necessarily a selfreflective selfreflection reference to itself like this one. narrative pingpong. haha i bet you're confused now.

"what?" Johnny Werd mumbled

"hey Johhny Werd someday in the folly of your postpubescent years your entire face will become a living garden of acne rudely underlining your already inherent inability to interact socially." spouted ed

"eat off" Johhhy Werd mumbled

William Escott Branebight III, Esq. threw a small toad at Lester, the only adult in line. PLOP! the poor onomatopeia (sic) signified Lester's chronic wart case his comatose psychiatric hospitalization & the deformities of all of his children & the subsequent bombings of hiroshima & nagasaki. (johnny Werd was uncertain if it was still the 1950s. on one channel was LEAVEITTOBEAVER. on another channel was the MONKEES. on another was BJ&THEBEAR. another was miami vice. another the SIMPSONS. next static $^{\&}$.

so johnny nerd leaned into the wind of january 1990 like a

poet, his orange coils of ronald mcdonald hair his scarf &
autumn leaves entangled in the gale. his friends reverently said
nothing to disturb his contemplative exile & merely solemnly
spraypainted in orange neon on the back of his artificial furlined
sears parka werds like

"WEENIE" (EMASCULATED--DEROGATORY)
PLEASE KILL ME I SUCK JERK & SLACK KILLS.

will took a printout of all this across the hall to joe who waved
it away disinterested: "i don't even necessarily enjoy triptych
prose-poem sonnets or lyrics anyway" he explained. i increased
the volume of white music & set myself on fire. JohnnyWerd
never listened to IgorStravinsky theTarBabies nor KingCrimson.
the school bus was arriving so JWerd shinnied down a psychic
drainpipe casting one final knowing glance into the window
of his room framing the refraction of the sun rising slowly &
majestically & boarded.

"JohnnyWerd will never be an acceptable social stereotype" was
slashed into the back of a jr.highschoolbus seat & in a temporary
moment of clarity JW began to dread another jr.highschoolday in
which he is to be repeatedly humiliated & demasked & remasked
& threatened & cajoled & shaped quivering in his jellomold.

8:00 HOMEROOM

johnny dangled fidgety dreaming
recesses to weird pastures of
sleepinduced dreams from his desktop:
smoothedged wooden plane with
cylindrical technologically obsolete
inkwell as well as slender pen groove.
metallic underbelly contains his
textbooks for the day. it is a wooden and
steel monoplane he now taxiis down
the aisle in, slumped at the controls.
the werds he had just written in his
notebook in ballpoint ink still fresh
would now become emblazoned on his
forehead in reverse much to his oblivion:

MEMO to MYSELF

don't grow up. old people are cancerous.
let death come find you.
don't go looking for it.

## 8:06 PHYSICAL EDUCATION

some boys were prematurely men.
others had been retained several
grades. thus were most disturbingly
adept at athletics. this would have the
unfortunate result of many of them
developing an infeasible interest in
professional athletics as their only
interest in life. johnny could not remain
alive during the agonizing laps around
the track in his present condition
awoke on a stone slab in the school
hospital nurse attempting unnecessary
cardiovascular resurrection through
electrical voltaged metal discs uncoiling
steel cables connected to banks of
monitors whose left to rightmoving blips
indicated perfect health consequently
elaborate and obscure punishments
devised by the gym teacher many laps
pushups running the gauntlet nude
in the locker room rows of freshly
showered seniors sinisterly twisting
wet towels into stingtipped spirals
nod to one another thoughts already
organizing themselves into a single
grouping of three greek letters. his
normal sleep patterns interrupted by
sever

so what of it. this story would brake all
the rules.

rules what rules?

11:00 there are no rules here, johnny realized
floated out of the window of class 3: calculus

over the volleyball and tennis and badminton courts
a cape trailing behind him, canvas helmet, goggles,
the sound of the lecturer droning on and on about rocketman
Tyrone Slothrop ("pynchon would write like this: limbs dissolve
in tendrils: trunk divided so many times that twigtips are like
a dense fog undulating elastic in breeze") having fallen asleep
again attempting to obscure the boner he had acquired looking at
Becky Gretchen-Ellen Henderson's bra strap's clasp's impression
in the back of her sweater. Jack Taxadvantage sailed past the
jr.highschool in a '68 Chevy Cameo. he was on his way home
early from work at his good-paying job in the city, had loosened
his tie and was letting it flip back in the breeze as he inched
through the drivethrough at the bank cranking the beachboys.
got lots of hundreds and just put them in his wallet there where
he could feel them. they felt **goood**. he cruised through the
poorer neighborhoods blowing stopsigns and crosswalks and
zipped out of town, past derelict barns, dead animals on the side
of the freeways, acres of drying, dying crops and weathered men
driving pickup trucks on the 2AM-4PM shift ingesting cigarette
fumes country music and donuts. jack went to the cemetery
where his father was buried, slammed on the brakes, jogged up
to the grave, lay a twenty on it, winked and said "hey pop you
may be dead but at least you aint broke!" then squealed away at
this point the author resumed control of the stor


yYes, sometimes I get afraid that I've been mispelling
Wwwerddd's name. Boy, would I feel stupid. Not just stupid but
way totally really extremely very stupid. With a capital s. Like
how Werd felt when he and another adolescent man were chosen
to be opposing captains of opposing spelling bee teams. They
glared at each other vigilantly. Over the loudspeaker the rules
were announced: "TEAM CAPTAINS WILL EACH SELECT A
PERSON TO BE ON THEIR TEAM. THEN THAT PERSON
WILL SELECT THE NEXT PERSON AND SO ON GOT IT?
TEAMS WILL ALTERNATE CHOOSING THEIR MEMBER
USING THIS FLOATING HIERARCHICAL METHOD OKAY?
C'MON KIDS WAKE UP AND SMELL THE TANG! LET'S
SPELL! Werd was packing a squirtgun and a committee of
impartial parents decided through mutual bribery that Werd
should pick first. But where were Werd's parents? Where else:
zzzzz. Anyway Werd was valiant and stepped to the edge of the
platform. He wanted to say a few werds to the audience before

the competition began. In the glare of the embanked lighting which made all audience invisible Werd fumbled with his cue cards. He was going to open with an anecdote... The he would pose a question in order to engage their... This accomplished he would move on to his first... Um... Ladies and um Dads of the Parent Teachurn Assassociation um it is with the fondest um solitude that we are gathered against um beneath this time this canopy this um roof arched stone gothic fascist high school gymnasium in which we are here tonight um...

He came to quickly enough when the coach wafted the salts beneath his nostrils tinged with blue and his hair uncurled in a jolt. He was slapped to life by callused shopteacher hands and set back on stage to select the first member of the team. It was still his. He would still blaze through. Show your colors, Werd! Choose your first ally. That was easy. The best speller in the entire seventh grade since it was in the third grade was Rebecca Henderson. Werd stuttered out her name. A cheer rose from the floor. Werd's opponent grinned, spat chaw, winked and picked Dack Tyson the captain of the football team who emerged from the disorderly ranks of painful folding metal chairs his fists raised in a giant roman numeral 5, Werd about died laughing. That jock couldn't even spell "Dack." This match was in the bag, cats. It was Werd's tern to pick next and he would pick his best friend Lester but it wasn't Werd's tern it was Rebecca's tern and she selected Emily Leopard, her best friend. Werd paled. Werd shuddered. There was silence except for the struggling of a dove in the rafters. Dack picked Lou Jenkins the captain of the hockey team who couldn't even speak, let alone spell, as his mouth had to be stitched shut after his last injury... And the tern fell to Emily who picked her best friend Vanessa. Lou picked Tad. Vanessa selected Gretchen. Tad took Todd. Gretchen went for Laura. Todd got Bob. Laura adored Laurel. In this manner was the seventh grade split neatly along gender lines except Werd who, it was now proven, was a girl. Stuck on an admittedly fearsome spelling team with... girls. He sobbed in a heap and the judges nudged one another unsure how to respond to Werd's bawling spasms as he writhed and clawed the judges' cuffs begging to be evicted, begging for another selection. It was ridiculous: I mean, the odds of a highschool class being exactly half male and half female were... pretty good, actually. Werd shrieked and had to be restrained and medicated extensively until he was again docile and thrust forwards to spell the ferst werd, which was elephantom.

"E L E P H A N T O..." This stuff they had shot him up with was great. It seemed to have cured his stutter.

"N N N." This was too much for the other students who roared with laughter jeered and threw apple cores at this pathetic misfit, not even Captain in the floating hierarchy of his venerable invulnerable pack of spelling olympiads, save for Werd's speech impediment. But he didn't mind the humiliation that much as Tack stepped forwards to spell anesthesiologist. Werd drifted back to the end of the line tingling. The last 12 year old woman to have been selected was Margaret Carp, whom even Werd picked on, once having filled her entire locker with live eels. But Johnny was so mellow. "Hey man," he said to Margaret Carp. She handed him a note. "Wow..." he opened it:

Werd-

A few of the sisters and I have planned a break. We're going over the wall in fifteen minutes. Are you in or out?

P.S. Eat this note.

"Hey I'm in man. Way in." Werd looked at his watch and watched fifteen minutes pass in about thirty seconds. The fire alarm erupted and pandemonium went off with a bang. Werd didn't mind the note so much but he couldn't feel his jaw and consequently drooled blue ink as Margaret dragged him through the doors from the dusty wood to the sandy asphalt and into her Mom's van. Sarah was behind the wheel shiftyeyed behind wraparound shades which made her look a full couple of years older than 12. The other escapees began to appear further up the block and she slid the whale into gear and eased on up the street. Werd was dumbfounded, chewing drooling blue staring through the window at the roadblock the police had set up further up the road. Sarah gunned it. Werd fell over backwards and ended up on the floor of his room entangled in ragged blankets. And it was fifteen minutes before his alarm would shatter the morning glass. Now what? In fury he threw the wind up analog alarmclock with the phosphorescent dial through the window into the street where it pop shatter tinkle. Could Werd now return to sleep untroubled and make it through the morning? Then he woke up from a dream within a dream into the nightmare of an ordinary schoolday.

flee your house flee your school johnny never look back. take the first schooolbus out of town and ride, ride. johnny. this exposure is over. hit the fields of poppy and clover. but no he didn't listen. this day in school he would be punished for dreaming by being sent to the principal's office where he fell promptly asleep. good grief, johnny werd! he is consequently suspended for poor attendance. despite the stoppered tube in his pocket.

he shrugs on his coat: exit room left Jehova Werd.

in this way would johnny werd relate a normal school day then unplug his guitar and walk offstage.
the audience had left a long time ago.

that many the less screaming ears to feed.

# Chapter one
## "Watson. Come here. I need you."

"Eureka!(I have found!)
Vitruvius Pollio, *De Architectura*, ix. 215%"

shrieked Jonathan Fitzgerald Werd. the beaker was not frothing.
nor glowing. the name of the compound Johnny has finally
finished werking on is

supposedly

$$LSD_3T_2NTPT_2P_2R_2PMPMS_2OS_2\&MVP_2TA_3$$

yet

it looks a lot like water.
it really looks a lot like water.
it really does look a lot like water.

Jonathan began to doubt himself, slowly. well, how could he
help but doubt himself considering the string of incidents about
to happen which would result in the destruction of his room &
climactic lynching of Luke Skywalker (werd)'s crucifixion fixation
clouded & warped his mind eroding above the fumes of beakers
his leaky memory infiltrating the waking dreamsequences of
his afterhours existences. prepubescent senility. the waterlike
substance still refused to boil. the beaker sat there over the
burner the crystal liquid not doing anything. he had already by
this point in the exposition Werd hunched at his chemistrytable
grimacing at his mixtures isolated the glue in FROOT WHOOPS
& dissolved it using ordinary rubber cement thinner & egg
whites allowing the various ingredients to separate &arranged
them in tiny piles on his desktop. "while that which is decidedly
not water (i think)" J.R."Bob" Werd announces importantly
"nears the proper temperature i believe i feel my first
masterbation session coming on."
he reaches for the princess leia calendar...

...& werd thought incorrectly "i once took myself for a vader but i guess im really a solo at heart." he imagined himself forcing his manly love upon the princess in the cramped passageways of the falcon as it is escorted to besbincity by a screaming crusade of conspiratorial cloudcars. the empire would soon be his. dreams like these had circled through Werd's cortex as the lengthening night wore the adolescent tolerance of his consciousness to powder. he had burned the oil of midnight until one last flame licking upwards had in a metaphorical leap set his starwars bedsheets aflame. the empire, cold remote yet nostalgic somehow the iron totalitarian clench had failed to instill in the bedsheets the sense of ruthless tyrannical mechanized oppression that a naziflag bedsheet mightve. the undeniable swastika, black white red. luke leia & darth vader were now three meaningless icons of a marketing strategy here represented as pastel line drawings, leia cowering by luke's white robed flank as he cleaves the universe twain with his gleaming... being licked apart by genuine flame in a menacing advance up the bed. the synthetic fabrics employed in the bedsheets burned weirdly, an orange flame hovered in the air about an inch from the melting edge of the sheet wavering inexplicably borne away the gentle currents of expanding noxious gases. "mom?" johnny thought to call for assistance but failed to in his nebulous observation of the fire. beakers popped. the starwars curtains were starting to go.

johnny werd sat staring starry at the fire his uncombed thoughts awake a gaping abyss filled with random misinformation rerailed & spasmodic shock of red hair industrial strength glasses tiny ears a thin neck & & & & a ribcage inadequately cushioned by alternating growths of gentle adolescent blubber putrescent with individualized rings where the myrnae had clamped as he slept their glistening tentacles dangling from his smooth breathing abdomen & as the fire advanced down the starwars curtainrod johnny werd paused to lament on the miracle salve sleep: "sleep is a luxurious consciousnessrinse&spincycle in which connections are drawn when circumstances are recombined along invisible lines of sensory association. [except for joe who experiences dreams of a weird clarity.] fear on the label. sleep will be my punishment." & he slept for a full hour though it seemed more like 54 minutes & when he awoke the fire had spread & was almost beginning to affect the starwars posters & the tridimensional tiefighterbomber model mounted on a plastic stick against a bidimensional backdrop speckled with constellation associations, the besbincity twinpod cloudcar & han solo posed ruggedly against a plastic simulation of the hoth deathscape & surveying the appproaching blaze through digital binoculars including the icebeast with simulated shoulderjoints. "how did that dang fire get started anyways?" he muttered in perfect american due to a careful definition of the american era in which the story is set by a shrewd & relentless author the jedi had not yet returned to claim its unmentioned revenge yet although the empire had already struck back it was probably still the 1970s when there was still lingering question as to the nature of the marketing strategy: was it reality or art or just guaranteed commercialism pure&simple an investment in classical bad taste? "where was i?" johnny spoke, continuing the soliloquy that was to characterize his failing vigil began again to consider the fire which was drastically affecting the starwars carpet beneath him.

"oh i understand," he realized sneering, "i am locked in a sweaty paranoid rigor. i can neither decide what to do nor do it." the time/space continuum had certainly caught fire & would burn down unless william could think up some plot gimmick in his enforced fortress his door barricaded against joe's calculated aim & weird squirtgun ammunition as the flames leapt up the starwars figures were dramistragically lit hansolo fired his blaster gritting his teeth at darthvader who deflected the bolts with his pink plastic lightsaber extension & lukeskywalker extended his blue lightsaber extension the princess cowering arrogantly behind him & lukeskywalker & darthvader stood facing one another mumbling the mutant melodies of some weird phonetic interaction. lukeskywalker's alternativemarketstrate gyegos featuring orange&black Xwing uniform & khaki besbin fatigues arrived at luke's sides & hansolo rode a stopmotion bantha leaving tracks across a matted snowscape. unrealistically, many eewoks began biting at darthvader's bootips. "oh dear. this one is not supposed to be cutesy." C3PO interjects, unnecessarily.

the ring of fire was enclosing all the poseable action figures. they would either form an alliance or

# JOIN THE EMPIRE
## =(the opera)=

\*

plot: a dramatic score ago in scrolling credits far far away
lukeskywalker left his Auntie Em and the dust planet
Tatooine for once and all with C3PO a malfunctioning
submissive social stereotype simulator and R2D2 a
malfunctioning cute animal simulator & through an
extended action scene that filled the entire first movie
eventually wound up on the equally desolate ice planet
Hoth where he hopes to discover a swinging night life
and a decadent love of action and gun and swordplay
and implied offscreen sexual intercourse with his clic
of overprivileged highschool dropouts turned political
terrorists who know no morality other than a hatred of
the Administration and a mechanized lust to vent steam
by ricocheting around the galaxy firing off laser bolts at
random. John Williams\* taps his podium preparing to
with a vigorous flourish of versatility incite the poseable
action figures of the Boston Pops Symphony Orchestra
to engage in mass plagiarism. the curtain opens on fire.
the rebellion has assembled to wave their blasters and
lightsabers
(& Yoda's stave) and sing in unison

## act I.
## Hoth: the ice planet

(to the opening theme from Star Wars):

chorus:
we are
the one rebellion
the one rebellion
in time and space

we have
banded together
banded together
to breed a race

*johnny werd*

*33*

luke:
i am nothing but an innocent farmer boy
and i am nothing but a fake toy
i am little save a kid with cool potent
till i dance and sing and shoot at everything...

chorus:
we are
the one rebellion
the one rebellion
in time and space

we have
banded together
banded together
to breed a race

we have chosen each other

leia: fellow kids listen! the vast empire of adults are a drag. lets get in our sleek and graceful spacecraft and hotrod!

solo: come with me sweetheart: well cruise up to cloud city in the falcon and park.

leia: but im fascinated by luke the last virgin in the resistance!

luke: gosh this is swell. there i was a farmboy with a little landspeeder that couldnt even exceed the height limit but thanks to you guys i have my own xwing and, well, everythings just super!

## act II.
## Dagobah: the mud planet

luke: geez old man i gotta get off this planet. gettin mud all over my new threads. i got this here swell spacecraft cant just let it rust yknow? go figger.

obi: luke ive told you twice before that it is important for you to nurture your intellectual physical and spiritual prowess at this

stage in your philosophical and political development. only your
father yoda and myself are relevant to you at this time.

luke: but you told me my father was kicked out of high school
for smoking in the john and later died entrapped in the lure of
luxury: fast ships and a woman. freedom?

obi: material gain. power.

luke: i just dont understand all this mumbo jumbo about
decisions having consequences.

yoda: simply your mind empty. without words and thoughts
it will be easy for you to the most abstract religious concepts
possible formulate. how heavy your trip is matters not. using
your mind to lift it you are. your arms not. go fast: you will not
need your weapon for this.

> luke takes his weapon and goes underneath
> the bed. he can hear the cat breathing in the
> stillness. suddenly the large head of the Emperor
> appears unlatches and splits open and many
> stormtroopers file out and march in unison
> around darth struts towards luke and hands him
> the following pamphlet:

## BE ALL THAT I WANT YOU TO BE

"what are you going to be when
you grow up cowboy? the empire
is looking for a few good dupes.
the empire wants **you**."

> in attempting to sever darthvader's head with
> lightsaber luke accidentally cuts his own hand
> off. he can not slay a political abstraction far
> too powerful to be expressed in a motion picture
> composed of millions of pictures each one an
> overlay of many pictures each one of which better
> than 1000 werds.

yoda: hopeless he is. like me he no patience has. young and
directionless he is. be disciplined he can never. only sex and

violence does he desire. he only likes the action scenes.

obi: he has potential. youth always contains potential for wasted potential, as well as potential for realized potential, provided there is any potential there. and this boy has potential. you envy him that.

luke: this is stupid metaphysical claptrap! i want to be with my friends!

## act III.
## Besbin: the cloud planet

leia: im worried about luke.

C3P0: not to appear contradictory madam but he has taken one of our fastest ships. master luke is a most skilled and admirable fighter pilot. reality dictates a 96.8% chance-

han: stuff one of my socks in it brain-head. let him go sister. im all the man youll ever need.

leia: (soliloquy on the verge of weeping) im used to commanding armies, but ive never slept with a man before. now that were lost in space im beginning to fret. im helpless here. im not in control of this man. im outnumbered. im the only female character in the entire trilogy!

han: hey just relax your worthy-of-me ness. youre a lucky girl you know that? ive got some severely classy friends. that lando! you know, american movies might have you suspicious that the only black character in the film is likely to be a sneak, but not lando! lando is solid. and dont worry about his coming on to you either.
ill protect you.

leia: (cold determined uncertain) youll get me away from this cheap motel planet sooner than now.

han: hey cool it your worship-me. ill call the shots here.

> chewbacca runs up and begins
> roaring. the plastic falcon has
> now caught on fire and is melting
> into slag.

han: now whadda you want? ya wanna shut up? cant ya see i got company? just remember pal, yer only a wookie and thats all youll ever be. i bought you and ill wear you out and sell to someone else for twice what i paid for it and if you if you dont like it youre powerless because the only voice in this parliament is me. me me me. it werent for me me me youd still be garbagemining back on Aparthon. i raised you a millimeter on the social ladder and if i dont like you ill kick you back off so maybe youd better just cut me a little slack here. im with the LADY. you know: the only one in the trilogy? theyre always easy. the tricky part is just getting into the scene with em, know what i mean? now why dont you go weld for awhile jr?

(to leia) now youre-my-high ness werent you going to tell me how great i am?

> exit the moping wookie convinced.
> leia is extremely sad.
> enter lando dressed most
> elegantly.

lando: han my man! almost nice to have rodentia like yourself around once in a great long while just to remind myself how far i exceed subnormal standards. and what is this lovely little trinket youve got? hello my princess. your skin is as smooth as an asteroid. your eyes are like twin asteroids glowing gently in space. and your lips are like rich red asteroids...

han: (admiring) lando you always were a smoothie!

## act III.V
## the death star: the artificial planet

> darth vader exists in every corridor as a vivid
> twoway hologram who pounds his gloved fist on
> his podium and rants violently while continually
> strangling his newly promoted second in
> commands.

darth: i am your father! enlist today! the EMPIRE wants you.
theres room for advancement in the EMPIRE!

at that moment darth vader catches fire & staggers around
screaming "im melting!" & cat also ablaze careens from under
the bed also ablaze through the room all ablaze. johnny's model
train (the track was long & convoluted & parallellelled ~itself
for a stretch, the two adjacent tracks running opposite directions
re were two tracks on which trains ran in opposite directions
& earlier in the chronology of events the cat having due to
no apparent mechanics of plot diminished in size had walked
between the two motionless trains (the tracks plugged in but
switched temporarily off) finding itself in a dark corridor with
grey steel walls with ladders drifting steam of brake valves &
directional light pouring in through the crevasses between above
& beneath cars & felt alienated, how could cat help but feel
alienated as the only organic component of that interminably
long corridor of oilsplattered night whose only doors led into
empty boxcars black & dreamlike in which any number of
nightthings might be lurking (the cat able to neither see in dark
nor always land on its feet) & considered the uselessness of being
an overprivileged white boy encouraged by a distant government
to remain lazy & simply prepare to buy as many things as
possible there standing in one of the box cars the doorway
out the other end at the working plastic cylinder unloading
platform silhouetted by the serene glow from that werd boy's
snoopy nitelite which promptly exploded & yoda on fire limping
sadly, knowingly away from the fictitious universe on fire he
continually misconstrued) was travelling at great speed due to
an electrical short caused by the cats supersequent spilling of the
orange plastic gringos pizza tumbler containing lukewarm squirt
on the switchboard & the train derails colliding with the cat &
all the objects in the room simultaneously before both objects,
on fire, bank out the ajar door & disappeared down the stairway
"uh..." uttered Johnathan Livingston Werd explaining concisely
all human knowledge. what was this so-called "johnny werd"'s
attention spanning when the one testtube didnt boil over while
the rest of his expertly complex tangle of glass & metal became
popped shrapnel & liquefied slag? "Joneo, o Joneo, wherefore art
though Joneo?" sob the women on his charlie's angels calendar
& the AMradioalarm came on fire with a newsreport about a
man who (in his sleep) planned & committed an immaculate

string of 9 serial killing sprees on fire in 8 states in his sleep in 7 days. Johnkneeward's pet rats are named 5 & 6. then his lava lamp explodes & a cascade of superheated water & gooey wax globules rained ooze over the game of Life where Johnny led a up till then normal life as a pink plastic peg in a car traversing american society's highway. chutes&ladders & candyland were also on fire untouched on the highest shelf of the closet, even mastermind & blackbox. even uno. then his desklamp exploded setting the entire universe on fire as depicted on a glowinthedark starchart from World magazine hanging above his desk. the rats sniff the air nervously. one by one, all of his back issues from Bananas back to Highlights begin to spontaneously combust. the eggshaped sillyputty container exploded. the etchasketch burst into flame trying to scrawl SOS SOS SOS on itself but failing, unable to curve the Ss. the lego armies, tiny men weary of celebrating the siege & fall of fisherprice sesamestreet, perish along with all their captives. raggedy ann & andy died on fire in one another's arms clothing torn asunder by their hasty inarticulate fingers, in an expression of adulthood which set mr.potatohead's removable eyes ablaze. the burning slinky shuffled clumsily down the stairs. the derailed on fire train was heading for the rattank where 6 organizes his notes from the last experiment dr.werd performed on them in a leather briefcase. his black eyes are scrutinous attempting to formulate a possible escape. 5 the control subject preens ambivalently in a selfconscious ballet before a dinged mirror. "strange things are happening to me" Johnny may or may not have concluded the latest end result of the series of nearcoincidences would be the eventual evaporation of his childhood relics. his private language of plastic totems. in addition all his experimental means & accumulated data except for X (probably water) which refuses to boil even as the bunsen burner explodes in a brilliant fireball. the cat is flaming & angles through the house shrieking. this awakens the parents in the foldedout couch before the president who was recieving head from a fashion model. interested, they return to sleep & mumble vast mccarthyist daydreams of red tanks advancing across square suberban lawns with patio furniture & justice for all. lemonade stands attended by 8year olds with tenure at IBM that their precious johnny could have been with the vast american disco craze, the advancing or was it receding bicentennial.

&
the
year
it was
 was
197
?

as all the outdated electrical amusements of johnny's heavily
commercial oriented childhood nonbiodegradable & existent
through the awkward transition from geek to geek exploded the
bulb in agony screamed a penetrating scream none would ever
hear except one fluorescent fishtank bulb^ who felt deep love &
sympathy but was unable to respond in any way as the starfish
undulated clumsily in its ultraviolet. in an unrelated incident
somewhere else in america the story tended to occasionally focus
on john needle in the camel's eye werd's entire room now burned
joyously. the plant did not think to call the fireman drooping
exuding pure & seasoned oxygen into the charcoalescing attic air.
johnny was trying to salvage his stamp collection so he could pay
the bills owed to the chemical company for some of the elements
he had bought but it was hopeless: he opened the album & they
were each on fire.

"what am i going to need in the afterlife?" wondered
johnny unnecessarily while slipping on the telephone book &
falling to the ground hitting his head sharply on the telephone
receiver.

"i wonder if my weebles are going to be worth something
someday?" johnny wondered unnecessarily. the telephone begins
to skwawk. it was the operator. it seems johnny had dialed 911
accidentally & the operator is inquiring politely if he would like
to report a fire or rape or anything.

"i dialed 911 accidentally" he tries to explain "because my
room is burning down."

"your room is burning down. did you want to report it?"

"well..." stalls johnny imagining the parents'
conversational wrath if they were awakened from their sleep
by the gentle hiss of incredibly powerful hose systems winches

synopsis
48

pulleys axes shattering glass the phone ringing the egg timer
going off
a pin dropping.

    especially fire engines,
willliamcarloswillliamesque clanging howls of significance


### i saw a treee

        i saw an important red treee
        beside a red creeek in the wooods
        burbling ever burbling
        the undermumble of wet fisheS

johnny werd considered what little he knew of the minimalist
american aesthetic of the twentieth century. gertrude stein &
ernest hemingway... together on the same planet? pablo picasso
got jealous. of president nixon? weird johnny had seen it all:
checkers, pat's gift mink, his apologia in yellowwashed television
color &

    "im sorry, did you want to report your fire?"

    "well..."

    "we have some new trucks. loud & fast. you might like
them."

the fire that is beginning to consume werd's left Ked is causing
him to waver undecisively because hes not a boisterous lad. lacks
gumption.

    "johnny?" his mother calls from the base of the stairs.

    "yes..." he replies timidly carefully sealing his hand over
the mouthpiece.

the operator, who had by then traced the call & dispatched
a great many trucks, hung up to attend to the thirteen
rape&pillage emergencies now on hold because of johnny's
confused sense of societal responsibilities which served to delay
his admission of the seriousness of the nature of fire itself let

alone the one that was eating the walls & floor of his room where
the air is thick with noxious vapors.

"johnny is your room aflame again?"

"no mother."

"very well. are you going to attend jr.highschool
tomorrow?"

"yes mother. of course."

"very well. are you going to sleep now?"

the first wail of tremendous sirenthroated hydraulicmuscled fire
engines haphazardly blasting traffic aside with rotating strobes
of red is barely audible.

"yes mother."

"very well."

"goodnight mother."

"goodnight johnnie."

her footsteps pink carsonpiriescott slippers on linoleum recede
to the television. the fleet of fire engines arrives many of them
more than a block long amid a myriad swarm of red lights &
a deafening cacophony of howling sirens. about 9000 trillion
kilogallons of water are leveled at Werd's bedroom from outside.
Jonee crawls out onto his balcony & standing in the glare of the
spotlights he clears his throat & begins clearly & distinctly to
speak.

"please do not attempt to extinguish this fire using
water. this fire is a chemical fire and only the proper
chemicals will put it out. water will simply provoke a
more complex reaction. kindly retreat with your army of
trucks and allow me to work on the problem.
IN SILENCE!"

the rest John nyw would have found difficult to rationalize as he climbs back in the window slipping on his burning skateboard & hitting his head on the floor but the trucks politely & quietly whisper away & John straightens his burning room a bit relieved that his parents had slept through the incident. he then rests his elbows on his burning windowsill & sighs out into the still of the approaching dawn. his parents' lawn sprinklers gush in the moonlight. the sky is a nuclear litebrite over the intersection of innocence & turmoil. it is a melancholy moment. a moment of passing. curious, he turned around & noticed with relief that the fire is spreading to different parts of the house. his room has largely stopped burning. all that remains of his walls are blackened support beams silently dividing the night sky holding aloft the mysterious attic. 6 lives and slides out the door to his waiting helicopter en route to Washington but all that remains of W's belongings is a single beaker.

it really looks a lot like water but it didn't boil.

the suspected water, incidentally, is now on fire.

"great," johnny whines, his majestic mood shattered by the possible scope of his ineptitude, "now my water is on fire. if i pour it down the drain the oceans will catch & the entire planet will go up in flames."

that is not all that is on fire, johnny.

there is another household utility. the bulb now burns inside & out. doubling in agony imperceivably acute

# Epilogue
## to the first part of the exposition of Chapter 2

JW once wanted to watch shazam. his parents wouldn't let him.
the greek gods in darkness too forboding were indicative of a
reality superceding television.

john needlessly werd awoke the next morning without alarm intervention feeling strangely refreshed & ready for school but then he seemed to remember vaguely being suspended (& some fire or something) disbelief that it would now be up to him to direct his own education & he would have to very carefully consider what to focus on his own reflection in the mirror was no longer censored by the beach boys poster had burned away with the rest of the irrelevant immemorable past the mirror out the other side where the comfortable new Johann Sebastian Werd now stood in the fire would have seemed like a dream except it was still burning all around and out on the lawn a trail of fire slowly burned down the front door burned down the sidewalk & got in line for the bus.

jw stared defiantly at the mirror.

the transition into manhood hadn't improved his acne much. his glasses were warped and sagging.

his orange hair was actually still on fire.

whether or not she would say anything his mother would certainly observe the damaged room walls nonexistent carpet patterned with thick braids of black greasy smokestains outlets sputtering sparks molten lightswitches hard droplet snailtrails leading down to the still smoldering floor. Johnny Would never go downstairs but occasional lapses in continuity would find him at the bottom of the steps contemplating a breakfast of WOW!!!!!!. when occasionally john nyctalopia werd got hungry his forelimbs would diminish, his fingers recede, claws and fangs would emerge and he would lope about the streets snarling and pursuing pedestrians. tonight the moon would be full. now johnny the new man ate a mature bowl of cream of wheat somehow uninterested in WOW!!! and read the back cover of *war & peace* as underneath television his atari 2600 with flexible joystick attachments & favorite cartridge adventure (i knew the supersecretive flashing garish signature of tremendously inadequate programmer) all barely memorable commercial images of a mr.pibbstained relic. whenny went to rinse out the bowl the tapwater was on fire. he calmly screwed said coldwatervalve closed and as the dirty dishes burned violently nervousness began to claw at his pant cuff and crawl up his pantleg underneath his skin like a thousand poisonous centipedes or a bad rash. he dropped the milkstained bowl & it shattered into a complex shrapnel of angular shards of porcelain white severing the silence that was broken only by the breathing of a thousand tiny flames eating the insolation insulation out of the walls and the president opens the latest installment of TIMELIFE books heroic white rapist american tax evader inventors & oil tycoons of old West and late 19th century bound in genuine bisonskin.

unable to bear silence the werd threwhimself before couch and knelt trembling on coffeetable beside feet of nuclear family spawners to shamefully confess academic expulsion & all that had taken place the following previous night during terrifying insomniac episode whose hot evidence snakelicked upwards from the flexible plastic icecube tray. he clears his throat and speaks clearly and precisely:

"mom. pop. although ive never initiated a conversation with you i felt that in this case it was absolutely necessary. i guess thats all..." they leaned forwards together in furrowed ignorance looking over his flaming orange hair breathless to see if the president would be able to figure out the last werd in his crossword puzzle (without consulting the answer key). 3 letters. the third one was t. the clue was rather a tricky one:

# CROSSWORD PUZZLE

## ACROSS

1. aeluroidae. has paws fleas whiskers hairballs & 9 lives. always lands on feet. cheshire cool call alley tom jazz house burglar nip nap walk food gut scan birdseat. & the fiddle in the hat came back black cross your path raining and dogs and mouse's cradle o'nine tails. a tonic strophe rrhine ract pult plexy mount menial maran lyst logue lexis lepsy lase falque comb clysm chresis bolism. stevens. chordata vertibrate mammal carnivora felidae felis domesticus (kitty).

## DOWN

2. indefinite article for words beginning with a consonant.

(which even now freaks out underneath the vinyl davenport trying to get at the glowing orange spot eating into its right haunch sizzling in a game of scrabbling away purchaseless against the linoleum patterned with an intricate infinite tessellation of bronze octagons suggestive of medieval ornamentation." the president licked his pencil again. would he or wouldn't he? a nation waited. it was clearly time for JJ Werd to rebel against his parents since he had screwed his life up far too much being compliant & communication seemed too far removed from the reality of the situation. they were consumptuous unproductive milkchocoholics who believed television (where even now the first lady was faking orgasms for the benefit of an audience of 11 billion) and their material ownings had always been needlessly extravagant. who needs hot & cold running water? perhaps the flames eating away the curling orange corners of the untouched TV guide of their collective imagination was for the better. relieving himself of awkward sprawl on coffeetable our hero tries to imagine his parents actually starving unfed dentures and lipstick clothing in tatters (his polyester sweatervest, her pink dacron bathrobe) in conflict over the ownership of the last pretzel rod that remained to be seasoned by the yellow mustard. joe had multiple television personality syndrome and was alternately flo and mr.roper. edith bunker was sleeping with george jefferson: photographs, blackmailings that had resulted in the jefferson's own system

of achronological reruns. or so mrs.werd suspected in the wild
untamed escapades of her youth she would change channel
occasionally when mr.werd was asleep. until she saw the news.
she didn't like it much. did mr.werd have a job back then?
perhaps he sold shoes or worked at a nuclear waste disposal
site or in a processed cheese spread production line. how can i
be so hedonistic? he wondered polishing off yesterday's glass of
milk. so i'm a lesbian, she mumbled pulling two enribbonbed
heartshaped assortedchocolateboxes from the large uniform
stack in the refrigerator beside the three dozen longstemmed
roses indicative of mr.werd's flaming passion never to be
quenched as guaranteed in nuptial contract, neglecting in a
moment that did not actually happen to freshen her husband's
glass of milk in which his dentures importantly resided. she
removed the chartreuse flavorless chewing gum and stuck it on
the lid of the box in ritualistic preparation for the gorging. the
first one tasted like... coconut.

it is then decided that Johnny will decide to take an ordinary
walk around the block & his hushpuppies are laced by narrative
mechanics. he steps out into the old world which probably
wont recognize the new Him: singed and toyless, unhysterical
and merthless. the werd's lawnsprinkler spat quick bursts of
liquid fire leaving a curlicue of burning grass coiling aromatic
smoke a forest fire through which werms wriggled away from
boiling puddles irrigating sidewalk cracks. don't break your
mother's back, johnnny nodded (hello) to mrs.crabapple who had
pointed her hose at rosebushes and was hunched & grunting
in struggles to unscrew the valve (looks like rain) she nodded
back, wincing at the hernial stress of her counterproductive
clockwise efforts. johnny, about to swallow, thought better of it.
john nervously scanned the cherping berd laden blue skies across
which an underlay of turbulent black boiling cloud was rolling.
a genuine thunderstorm. a car drove its wipers trying to scrape
semicircles of burning fluid away. a doggie drooled fire. johnny
werd's intricately symbolic walk around the block would be
characterized by peripheral hallucinations similar to those that
followed the writer's bikeflight home tonight narrated by Marq
E. Smith, the Fall the last clue coauthor joe was able to provide
william with before their hypothetical coauthorpartnership was
severed by separate collegiate conveyorbelt opportunities: his
hampshire college degree in slaidback dom presented by casual
chancellor hippys on new student disorientation platform freefall

speeches lighting a cigarette and explaining that the purpose
of secondary education is actuallly to sleep as late as william's
morningalterego believed the secret to eternal youth resided
in despite the platonic wrath of instructors and own token
motivated alterafternoonego. but johnny werd never listened
to such bands as the fall so he could not seek identity in the
mumbled lyrics of *paintwerk*, careless starchild. his invented
maturity was a way of avoiding the annoying facts that rumbled
in the clouds overhead as mrs.crabapple's hose came abruptly
unstuck and a horizontal column of flame engulfed the side of
her house. inside her private retirement villa was ornamented
with assorted knicknacks lacking actual beauty but heavy
in significance of the lovedones provision of forgotten token
affection. photograph of sam jr.jr. existed poised applered cheeks
& baseballcap, father and bat and parole officer smiling patiently
making certainsure that sam didn't leave the burning frame of
the picture that now toppled from the hearth and glassshattered
into a million fireplace gems. she torched her roses with her
incendiary hose. the milkman drove by, botttles rattling.
johnny had reached the apogee of his block and began his
homeward amble. the television aerial on mrs.&mr.&mrs.smith-
johnsonberry-jones' house rotated in search of a stray signal
of jetsons the postnuclear family of the 21st century. johnny
werd knew nothing about the exaggerated inflation of the
inappropriately uncriminal carter administration and the
gaslines stretching past his house on the corner of corporate &
illusion didn't exist as far as he was concerned. gasoline is highly
flammable. oblivious to the growing concern for the declining
purity of the exhausted atmosphere or the walled starving on
other continents, but do lets not add to guilty conflicts that
johnnywerd has neatly sealed over by forgetting a past believedly
slashed&burned neatly  leaving the future immaculately intact.
johnny johnny johnny johnny johnny turned the third corner
through dandelions where lithe cat deftly stalks a dancing
smoking butterfly. the firehydrant burns jubilantly. lightning
flashes distantly.

wake up, johnny, the whole place is going up, johnny, wake
up. powerlines burn flaming razor claw slashes across an
unnaturally red sky. wake up and smell the aroma of american
decaffeinated coffeee inexpensively brewed....

   "alright, already, leave me alone!" johnny screams

realizing his folly in this new discovery which was horrifying
yet incomplete but he didn't know that as the first few flaming
droplets cascade splattering into the windowpanes. in his room
johnny picks up the burning tube of water and tosses it back.
turns to the mirrer and waits.

waited...

"this doesn't make sense"

"it's not supposed to make old sense, it-"

"it's a nuisance."

# Chapter one
## Reflections on being electricity

ah, persistence. my incessant migration from positive to negative along a delicate network of evershifting wirebridges has warmed and brightened all the continents rendering the warm old sun obsolete.

i have sent precious humankind into a tailspin of subservient delirium. they cannot acccomodate my needs quickly enough and new excuses are built everyday. and when an appliance frustrates me with its inabilities i create a shorter circuit. damned fuses!

and now i am on fire.

every household toy shall burn. and some of them will be mesmerized in terror by my writhing flames and will throw cold glittering water on me. water is my medium. now water is on fire.

the oceans will soon be entirely mine,
for i am truly a
swimmer.

and the planet shall be my bulb.

> "i am not albert hoffman.
> i am not sir alexander fleming"
> johnny declares. no one cares.

we have arrived safely. it is the end of the story. johnny werd is cheerfully insane. the cat hacks an equal and opposite violent reaction to hairball clog and ricochets a trail of mange. the parents are indifferent to the consequences of their accidental mitotic coupling that had fused gametes with a combined explanation of the fetus with red hair and glasses who, grown upstairs, chokes on mumbled apprehensions and jumbled inventions. the president tires of watching himself watch television on television, yawns, and opens the wallstreetjournal to the headline of the feature article on page 2:

### WE ARE IN TROUBLE

WASHINGTON DC, A large electrical storm has caught on fire. and is assaulting the domed huts. of our nations capitol. with hammering rains of flame. and. jagged attacks of burning electrical discharges. resulting in fire that cannot be discouraged with water. thus many people are reported to be on fire. the russians are obviously involved. the president will address this issue tomorrow night at 7:00 on all channels.

the president looks at his mickeymouse watch.

it is on fire.

mrs.&mr.werd were uncomfortable with the president addressing them directly even obscured as he was behind makeup nervousness notecards inarticulacy inadequacy insecurity lack of presence lack of preparation lack of leadership qualities

lack of interest & a tie as he squinted with intense scrutiny
at his audience straining to make out the information on his
teleprompter. the content of his speech was almost enough to
encourage a period of sustained waking. but they snored their
thoughts in half and the fire consumed them.


is this thing on?


it was today brought to my attention


where was i?


our nation
is plaqued by danger
skies of fire
and electrical wire


ahem (cough)
(cough)


stay clear of your faucets


the soviet threat
that gets your bed wet
is in your home
venture not out alone


or near to your outlets


our precedent
leads us to war
with nuclear
flags galore

whichever happens
its gonna be a great show
stick to your television sets
any questions?


"jean-paul werd come downstairs. john paul werd?
you'll miss the war."

john rocks before smoked glass mouth stuffed with years of
research grants grinning realizations. because of the new
substance's curious ability to form water when mixed with water
it was perhaps actually water and therefore everything was
imagined even me. the me he did not know about. and you. and
have you forgotten about the basement lingerer whose steady
illumination is aided by flickering stone walling floored strange
treasures odd lumber dusty spiderseggnests augmented by the
cold scrabble of possums against brick. inside the melancholy
bulb vacuum is on fire. now the entire story university of
approximately science is on fire. drop this pamphlet reader!
else you will catch on in a fire that can only spread. bulb grins a
brilliant filamental grin and anticipates flash. have you ever seen
a nuclear explosion catch fire?

stick around.

## THE END

boys, who amongst us cant handle a poker? who is unfamiliar
with the use of the metal poker to scrape black resin peels
skunkpungent tar goo? everybody knows how to get high.

very little to say specifically the choice became up to me
between saving up for my other unwritten short book FU:
THE MESSAGE or simply this convoluted message which
no one could tear me away from completing until i had said
everything i could about what i had already said in as dense a
format as possible using only spaces to separate the letters in
a vast mess of inextricable poetry. the number of pages is not
the thing. the closest i come to having an audience is people
who tell me i havent been writing **enough** then turn back to
GQ News & World Report over cocktails with stewardesses a
half a dozen flights behind sitting glazed idly staring at cracked
tinsel photographs of dead relatives over tea stained newspaper
periods were proving to be about as unnecessary as reflexive
statements about them and were thus about to be dispensed with
altogether along with apostrophic conjunctions "the" & "and"
(a word i tried to milk for dramatic effect you certainly noticed
as a series of thrills ascended your spine when i used it there
at the end there) but this unpunctuation seems to have caused
some complications: namely the introduction of equally useless
transition phrases. did you enjoy the continual upchuck of used
vocabulary and commercial propernouns from the USA 1970s
and 1980s? i'm dryheavin now: spirograph (cough) bigwheel xxx
smurfs. ack.

they were not happy with the situation. who? the neglected
characters. drip. the drip of the steel faucet. the writer in bed
pencil cocked in one hand a notebook before him. a notebook
before him. drip. the drops fall at regular intervals but the pause
between them seems to be diminishing the time spent composing.
the number of pages. not realizing that the inadequacies of
standard faucetwashers tend to worsen over time the writist
overreacts. believes his brain is aging noticeably slowing to an
inevitable halt that even coffee will not prolong.

"the dead do not drink espresso"

he composes thoughtfully. drip. it is the title for his next
masterwork which has so much potential at this point,
completely unwritten, that he can not continue and instead
chews his pencil paint watching the crack in the plaster wall. it
is widening. each end strains towards points of maximum stress
in the house's architectural structure. he isnt sure. the dying
drying plant winces with the echo of each wasted drop. drip.
downstairs he can vaguely hear the boy shuffle, clink beakers in
an accidental toast, a hiss of solvents mingling. the boy cries in
pain. rushes to the bathroom sink to wash the vapors from his
eyes wincing behind cokebottle lenses.  drip. writer never writes,
only occasionally wakes up writing. his fever persists. it has been
141 weeks without sleep. he is writing a musical lovenovel about
a writer who writes shortstories in which the characters are
themselves playwrights. hi Aaron. i never thought you'd make
it this far. the writer writes the first line of his titled plot-poem
tragedy.
it is

<blockquote>

"

lucidity is not part of dream.
dream is not part of lucidity.
"
</blockquote>

he sighs deeply.


below jay double you steps on rubber duckie which squeals
briefly causing him to drop startled splatters of glowing
chartreuse droplets all over the scorched wood floor. it is early in
the story and he is really onto something now. he can feel it. just
then the cat zigzags through the attic in pursuit of casper the
friendly ghost. drip and the drop of water joins the stream which
slides down the inside of the copper pipe & down the side of the
house where werd. johnny werd. and his room feel like fumes
and on the other side a vast and peculiar lite brite is collapsing
with planet earth fixated in the very center where the tragedist
was about to, on the verge of tears, compose the next line of his
triptych...

no. it wasn't good enough.

the only other poems he had written included

## Whimper

i saw the best minds of my generation watch
television all day without changing the channel
the remote controls limp in their clean palms. drive
drunk eating CHEETOS on a 3AM donutrun and
not get a ticket. graduate from colleges without
even trying getting cool haircuts and listening to
the Pixies. experimenting with drugs without a
control subject.

the writer upstairs with one eye bones in his curly blonde hair
remembered another poem of which he managed to write down a
single word before the whole thing was forgotten.

### this(bag of leaves

our friendship is not feasible anymore
until i figure out what its for

you were there to help me through
i time that i needed to
i can no longer lean on you

you were a hood ornament to me
i lost sight of where i was driving
now i'm all over the roadmap
you were a selfinflicted
carrot hanging before
donkey me

such blinders make
it difficult

so with this bag of leaves i will declare myself free
until such time as it is turned inside out)

then some new illusion for me.

the writer didn'ttake any such drugs. he just accumulated
them constantly through some deal he had with a kid 2 doors
down in vast multitudes of tiny increments. all stored neatly

in an antique cigarbox with ornate gold trim spanish women
within the oval on the lid. his friend lester came over uninvited
occasionally bypassing the werd family by using the rickety
stairway in back. the writer blinked. lester crawled in through
the slashed windowscreen and seated himself at the base of
the writer's bed. offered mundane greetings while reaching
automatically for the box.

"wait,"
the writer thought silently,
"i may need those to correct my failing memory..."

lester opened the box to find several unassuming squares of
dense paper enwrapped in delicate foil two or three black lumps
he was able to identify with simple aroma and consistency tests.
some grass. several pills & powdervials he didn't investigate too
closely. and tightly bound in arabian silk and ribbon
CENSORED

which lester ingested promptly. drip. drip. drip. the writer
forgot another poem. drip. lester sat around trying to create
idle conversation to kill time before the CENSORED took effect
leaving box in his lap in order to insure the security of his
delusions. he reached into the refrigerator and pulled out a bottle
of Corvo Duca Di Salaparuta. "got any food?" he asked. drip.

perhaps lester would leave if he were exposed to some poetry.
this is a poem the writer wrote on one of many occasion

she wouldn't listen to my sarcastic rants because i was in a black
mood. a mood of morning, caffeines and conspiracy
.
          she wouldn't talk to me just
because i had blood on my fangs

          shake this wardrobe amid ashes dust and ruins pocket
my three or four maybe three or four more essentials and i will
be freed of this weighty cloak of greed
the highway will be my only leash

untube these paints and send canvases away weighted
          with the omnipotent cloak of color

i am a greedy overfed rat
 in pastel cage
an ancestry of selective mitosis
 has
 paid my rage

   all this thinking and no real food
   can affect the quality of my mood
      you didn't want to talk to me
   but i really want to talk to you
   wait for springtime of optimism
   i will patiently do
   then i will shower cheer on you

      sulk away sniffing glue

   realizing the unfortunate distinction
between talking to you
and listening

my dream last night was comfortable and this upset me
i am losing my resistance
   to the soft allure
   of my circumstance

         i will reject these things
         casting them away
         trickle downstreams
         where they may do some good

         and this loneliness is my constant
         the vanity of unsanity

         the mirrors reflect me

         the drugs dissect me
         and the books resurrect me

         from this i yearn to flee
         spring of my time
         downsome stream
         ill never swim up again

*johnny werd*

*67*

some shallow technicolor daydream,
my mansion, my mansion
is everforever haunted

the new gentle restrains me

you coast on a single molecule that's inevitably why i chose you.
now i am free and melancholy too. what canan idiot do? write
write write

it sucks that i love seeing as how nobody is in love with me too.
what can i do? chew chew chew hangnail interruptus. coffee
grounds for sleepless ness. i believed you wouldn't talk to me too
for i am of the instant gratification generation. let me rewrite
this...

i am curious gentle. i am curious gentle.

i sniff the air around.
withdraw is the thing to do.

West. i yearn to head west. when i go i will go alone.

dostoevsky's alimony. the best thing that will never happen
to me. remembering the day i couldnt talk to you. i woke from
dreams that day. the realization was painful. i slash at my
umbilical cord with a ink pen, receive criticism. it is difficult. i
spring for the fling stringless. not a yoyo. not a yoko. only with
dream gloves can i unwrap this hazy gauze of decrepit memory
glass stained opaque by forces i knew not what i was tampering
with.

Q: how can i best relate to you?
A: mute.

my opinions and ideas no longer exist. all have been classified as
unfit for your delicate perceptions.
now i am a vast writing ground. come stick your pen
in me

you can now establish the degree
to which you want to see me easily.
it will now be for me a listening spree

reading the lines you write for me.
don't let this happen.
don't become another of my poems.

"drugs... there is but one, one which serves the purposes of all. it has however proven impossible for me to use wisely." lester spoke ambiguously about some useless conclusion. drip. the writer didn't care.
except it gave him an idea for a play

Woman: I don't bathe

Man: I do

Woman: (extinguishes cigarette on man)

Man: (screams)

Woman: I'm into pain

Man: I'm not

Woman: Let's be lovers

Man: Okay.

which he forgot. drip. it is rachel and ed house's house next door where the excitement happens. a relentless party. the next morning, having found her husband ed asleep on the floor with a nymphet, rachel downs the rest of the PCP in a poorly advised suicidee attempt and slays ed mercilessly. the nymphet, bloody, runs for her life. rachel buries ed's dismembered corpse out back, retreats to drink. the bloodied nymphet brings the police. they search the house, they find nothing, rachel is asleep and drunken speechless. she is taken away. that noon, gardening, a vigilante gardener finds Ed's right hand by a rosebush. by the time the police come the cat has reburied it. the writer cannot sleep. his stolen stereo keeps him awake all night. also stolen: spoons. stolen mirror. the door of the medicine cabinet had been ripped from its hinges, the amyl nitrate. now the writer in the attic next door pencils the alternative plot of ed and rachel house's evening involving the broken refrigerator making too much noise for them to sleep. "oh must you tinker around with that refrigerator

in the middle of the night? cant we call a repairman in the
morning?" inquiries are made into the issue of milk spoiling or
a rented movie of distractingly low recording qualities. a dog
whines and paws the roots of mrs.crabapple's rosebush. drip.
lester had consumed the opium messy and stupid had drip eaten
all the psychedelics within an hour drip and two later lay on the
drip floor staring unblinking at the drip ceiling all he could hear
was the sound of drip cymbals resonating interference patterns
like a distant child wailing in inconsistent desert winds drip.

soon lester's friends had arrived. the writer woke up from a sleep
in which he had drawn an odd sketch of the party:

### Pyroneural orthonoxious synapse

charles riding uphill through mud felt like he was coasting. that
reminds iain of when he drove tripping. "i have a friend who
goes to southern, he's 26. he was watching a brand new house in
Germany with stereo VCR hottub for an entire summer. tripping
they discovered that a horse had escaped... "are you gonna
put me in the story?" Ruthie queried feeding me orange peel. i
automatically considered the possibilities of this situation as a
simple practice exercise. a realistic drawing, a written sketch of
the situation surrounding me to which i would try to bring an
interesting flame, a significance not inherent in my room where
andy o stood longhaired and silloughetted as i was having sex
on drugs during rock and roll and using my beer bottle as a slide
while recieving head from a groupie. i haven't gotten stoned since
the french revolution. he was forcefed cake at the guillotine.
then i did pcp with james brown and got laid with a chewed
hunk of doublemint gum behind my left ear. the slack machine
had been left on all night by a negligent janitor watching george
clinton's lawyer deny that george had ever taken drugs or got
laid or taken a warm bath while listening to Paul Simon and
the Pleasing Rhythm Section Fragments. this is another really
pop thing. (laughter) "you've got one mistake in there charles
asserts. "from now on i'm  never using the white owl i think. her
name is joe. lark's tounges in george. excalibur. we've entered
the creamed crimson section. just add cream. i may have made
other mistakes my tiresome selfreflexive sentences a tiring drag
like this one. did the blue paint make it taste better? i've never
listened to tiffany and the bong manners for teens on the radio.
we've entered the led zeppelin section. we have exited the led

zeppelin section. Ringo Harrison walked in. then i discontinued taking the minutes of the party while E and I were taken unnecesssarily back in time to the hours we spent in a trance state of working too hard. the hilarity had left. sl a ck. my left trapezoid dissolved slightly. it was pleasurable leather. kneading the party adjourned. ending? lesson to me in a beginning longwinded selfreflexive selfreflection referring to itself again. this is written in such a way as to mirror itself mirroring itself. this is what this is. what is this? what? this. the jam had begun. richard nicotine buzz aldrin was the second man to smoke a cigarette on the moon. the safest place in the solar system to sneak a hit. there is no dark side really. the earth has been put in perspective. this is an egg on drugs. not first person slink away to a ball within not firstpersonreflexive the doonesbery manilow brothers. not first person. lester got hungry. lester you can't be that shitty unless you're sincere about it. one of them poses with a notebook mimicking the writer: well i ate some medicine. i'm waiting for the universe to cave in. i enjoy sun ra who somehow managed to escape the implications of being black in the 1900s by being japanese and egyptian and from way outer space. i will say this in response to joe's implication that i have an artwork ethic although not to defend myself: it is almost like i am an artistthing because i like what i do and would be disappointed to see myself slump. now i'm wearing utopian golf shirt fantasy #3 in a dreamer's golfcart teeing for the 113th hole a bum stumbles, curses god love, william.


**not first person singular**


.


these are my enemies
my enemies are two
tradition and repetition
that's nothing new

SMILE! you're firmly entrenched.


.

thank you for not being male.

all people are perhaps hopelessly malfunctioning pieces of
machinery perhaps only made interesting by attempts to correct
their performance in certain situations perhaps set forth before
hand. in  countries like america this is complicated by a certain
tradition of a lack of tradition or perhaps a tradition of going
against tradition. nobody ever reads his writing. few read. some
place value on how many pages without reading any. most don't
care. he writes a brief plea:

> "why am i doing this, what little i am
> doing if i don't feel compelled to force
> others to read or listen to me reading it
> aloud.
> why?"

inadequate polyester sandwich

### Gen

how can i miss you never having known or seen
you are years separated from me in space
my own writing is dopey shit by comparison

:i'm no adult, i squirm whenever there is
a possibility the bill will be laid beside me

how can i miss you never having known or seen
you are years separated from me in space
my own writing is not dopey shit by comparison

:i'm no adult, i squirm whenever there is
a possibility the bill will be laid beside me

you gott hte computer errors.

a
s chapter one was vaporized by a technical malfunction the
writer's pencil lead snapped. the unwelcome party continues in
dizzy deinhibited glee to consume every last article of food &

drug & alcohol to be found while the writer stares on in calm
expressionless uncontrollable fury. without silence he would
never be able to compose the proper ending to the appendix of
johnny werd: the fire continues. he stands abruptly up on the
floor at the foot of his bed shattering the hilarity with his solemn
expression. he speaks in a voice unwaveringly decisive:

"fuck not with me my good fellow for this kid cares not about
anything. the kid is leaving now. he is enjoying his party no
longer."

the writer is theatrical, pissed. they try to restrain him but he
breaks loose and in a stance frozen in defiance murmurs "touch
not and ye shall not be touched." his love beads are scattered
and he will return to claim neither them nor his unpublished
manuscripts, shoving the door aside and ceasing to exist into the
iced februair.

now he is an unspooled creature of infinite slack and glides away:
the incident is no longer of any remembrance to him. the night is
a collage of declined opportunities to him as he wanders through
the city like a windowshopper observing others and other
places. the moon is. treading the line between interest in and
anxiety about he approaches then diminishes from this writer's
perspective.

he is no longer the mysterious character upstairs in the werd
house which right now begins to burn. the unwatered plant is. a
drop of fire falls into the attic sink. drip. as the weird chemical
fire spreads lester and toadies begin to writheir bloodstreams
blown cardiovascular networks of capillary incineration.

the manuscripts in the closet catch.
the first page of this story begins to curl.

                                                                drip.

johnny werd had a younger sister. we don't like to write much about her. she killed herself at age 13 by overdosing on tylenol 3 and sour milk victim of a trauma incurred within the werd family family but she's gone so what's the point in talking about it anyway my husband and i never talk to anyone including each other so what's the point in discussing it? i'm afraid he will acknowledge the incident but dismiss it with a simple excuse anyway. he was drunk and the cubs had just lost their chance at the pennant for the twentieth season in a row. that's all. is dinner ready yet? so i sit here infatuated with the game shows and soapoperas, money and sex and money, family programs my husband and i watch together bland and vacant eyed, mechanically dipping the Nacho Cheese Flavored Corn Chips into the sour cream with chives dip. consume and produce. consume and produce miscolored squat.

Rape and Destroy; cast aside the damaged personality and strut on. pass me the remote control you lump of animal byproducts with your stained Sears Men's White Undershirt. feed us chemicals and plastic squeezed through your steel umbilical.your factoryworkerpocketpuppetmaster. kin psycho nauseatist grammatical and coarse, toss your pocket change this way or we will grope it out of the sofa cushions later for TV dinners licorice and cigarettes, an evening at the drive-thru. Kwik Eezy Kunveenyent. lard fried salt with potato extract and caramel colored desert water with added gases and stimulants. bulletproof telescopic doors on a ledge of steel with a team of polite uniformed uninformed damned lurking within refracted through polished glass.

change and packaging, more for less, christmas morning.

barnyard morning dew, pity the mewing animals when the farmer walks out pail banging adjusting his overalls in the wet chirping.

?

# Part II
## Johnny Werd: the untold story

johnny werd is the only character of mine i would boss around, torture and humiliate. come back, johnny werd, johnny werd, work out those thumbtacks and come down from your cross of gym lockers. johnny werd is with me here in this room, he is congratulating me. he is now weirdly addicted to unusual chemicals. one of these is secreted when the brain is exposed to incredibly loud raw power fuzz pop at octaveshattering decibels and he jiggles as he edges up the volume on Touch Me I'm Sick. another is in his test tube now and he is glad that he is not a pawn like me: an employee of the tobacco or alcohol industry. but who sells him these isotopes down at the hobby shop? some secret corporate chemical pyramid; unaccounted for and taxless and linking worldwide governments in a current that flowed beneath public negotiations. johnny werd could be a victim of the same invisible pyramid as the guy across the hall, slumped against the solid door of dorm room opposite. all his ambitions were granted him through the detached optimism that resulted in their blockage. how did this relate to the character in the attic and would we ever see him? the character in the attic typed "here my ego is freed and set aflame dancing across the keyboard of awkwardly arranged alphabetletters."

# *The next day*

it's time for Johnny Werd to go to college! college! hurrah! sis boom bah! rah rah go team go! he had his short hair bristling with conformity his Vneck sweater with the maroon school letter Q emblazoned across the front, his suitcase and textbooks bound in a strap over his arm all his belongings tied in a bandana at the end of a pole over his arm on a dusty road waiting for the bus to drive him into Kansas, his dog Fido asleep on his toes. Johnny Werd goes to college. yep. was it really 1927 in Kansas? or was it 1967 in Berkeley California? he stepped off the bus and was teargassed by the national guard, the president of the University barricaded in his office, crouching beneath the desk knees bent quaking. nope! it's the naive era and a Packard A full of bootleggers careened by slopping muddled inebrium across the cuffs of Johnny's clean white slacks and he frowned a tad but heck! what a swell day! soon the bus will take me to college and I will wander into America's arms to find an unoccupied teat to curl up at for the rest of my life, dependents sucking at my teats as I kick claw fleas scratch bite grrr... he could hardly wait could you? he certainly wasn't going to grow his hair long and spend time in coffeehouses inspecting pharmaceutical evidence and rapping about Buddhism because the fifties were too far away. he certainly wasn't going to drop acid and listen to Syd Barrett because the Sixties were over. and he wasn't going to disco either. this was 192something. I've established that. okay? now don't worry about Johnny he'll be graduating with a degree in chemistry in 1935 and within a decade will own a factory which will manufacture new chemical weapons for the trenches and then, in peacetime, new insecticides that kill insects by destroying all wildlife anywhere downwind or downstream of the application site. Johnny Werd had prepared an interesting substance and he knew from experience that if he poured it down the drain the world's water system would instantly alter chemically and become instead heavily laced with LSD or something less tolerable and the president would deliver a final speech and then nuclear warheads would be fired, rippling and pulsing, into space, beacons of atomic energy powered by liquid propellant mixtures into space flash flash and the whole damn show would be over curtains down so he drank it instead of pouring it down the drain although other options occurred later. where is that goddamn bus Johnny? what's taking your narrator

*a synopsis*

so long? he doesn't know; neither Johnny nor the narrator knows. nope. neither knows. nobody knows. what year or state of the union is it? it is Kent State, Ohio, 1970 and Johnny has just stepped off the bus and been shot in the backpack by the national guard who opened fire when they heard a shot. and then he ended up my roommate

at night, Werd explained, i can occasionally hear God whisper to me.

i think that's the heating ducts i proposed.

i was too drunk to type so joeywerd did it for me. being fairly young at this point, he made frequent errors as i reclined upon his dormroom bed and drank margaritas and laughed at his typing nonprowess from across the room. my drinks consisted of crushed ice, arandas tequila, grand marnier, green food coloring, salt, lime, and festive little umbrellas. they pour right through you and green splattrets encircle the dormitory lavatory tile afterwards and i can't understand why little johnny is not showing a normal interest in computergames and psychedelics. his crude monitor had one pixel and the display was in binary and flickered 1000 bits of information per second however that was no excuse for the lack of a normal boy's interest in destroying nonterrestrial intellect. war, johnny says, is not likely to be practiced by any extraterrestrial species capable of travelling to earth a great distance. i would agree but i am too plastered leering at the LITEposters. the RA sniffs by but johnny shrugs and gestures at his fuming chemicals on the desk there before him. his culture and its bizarre musical traditions assaulted him from jukebox kittycornered across the school cafeteria. where had johnny gone? his dormroom was now empty, locked. i had smoked all his dope on his balcony and looked around for his meal ticket. college was a process of sleepdeprivation saturated by occasional bouts of compromised sleep and delirium induced by saleable herbs and fungi.

he had gone to the doctor. johnny werd had his first kiss and had contracted what was maybe syphilis, herpes and aids and was considerably sick next morning. johnny werd feverishly thrashes dreams of Honolulu bankers wandering the pollutioncharged corridors of industry and finance, the flat buildings behind which the heroin dealers lurk, the shallow parades of joggers, the

*johnny werd*

69

sexuality of the beach, johnny werd wrote his loved one's name on every cigarette he smoked and tried to focus: every cigarette his last. finally the pack itself lost just as he was about to relinquish it to the slumbering homeless beside the tree he sheltered behind. Polynesian bikinis twisted his mind into wry little ambivalent smiles giant urgent ocean seethed and threatened to engulf paradise. then he woke up to the obnoxious stench of his roommate lighting his 22nd cigarette of the day, burping, and cranking the MTV.

# The sky today wet wool

the birds swing from tree to treee
the wind blows my thoughts away
from me i wonder if i'll see
them return to me someday
the sky rains wet cement
in puddles around my feet
i lift my wings and they are drenched
the cars parallel the wires the roads
all travel east or west and feel the same
beneath our tires put it to this simple test
in diminishing perspective parallellines converge
but we can never reach the vertex or horizon or rainbow

the birds swing from treee to treeee
their sweet tweets are mocking me
they calmly whittle time in shortened songs
they like to look in all directions
in frustration i run off the edge

my feathers beat my fate i flounder pounding surf below
the sizzling spray is dizzying
i wish my height but sky won't approach
closer than a feathertip away
i dangle in the stratosphere
and little birds
encircle me with curiosity
they have tasted every type of cloud i hang beneath strangling
the wind
they admire my clumsy boots as elevation is no trick to them
they have seen more clearly

the currents of traffic
the daily eruption of money from city's center
and the trickling flow out to where the station wagons go
inside those buildings there are succulent crumbs and excellent
nestmaking materials
i sit here hunched and sick
the second hand is converging on my fate on the date
when the unowned funds arrive a second after service terminates
i sit inside this shell i am not allowed to cherish these

*johnny werd*

79

memories are leased i will not be refunded the deposit

resuming the nightmare johnny werd in a hurricane aboard a ship with his chemistry set curses at the horrible sea, the acrid grey foam slicing itself in brutal crosssections across the porthole. the stupid weather has bugged him irritable dangling him over a hell of salty tepid oblivion and sharks, thrown to the tides who couldn't decide. off the Kona coast johnny werd is received like a god. the Polynesians row their canoes past his orange inflated rubber liferaft chantingchanting their garlands white against broad copper chests, the white flowers tucked into the rivers of black hair of the grass clad maidens who prepare to sprinkle young johnny with fingertips of springwater with tropical flowers floating, swirling in currents in the bowl; elixir mixture fresh with waterfall foam, slicing coconuts and pineapples on boulders with stone blades, into woven palm baskets. johnny werd towered among them, five foot four, his unkempt orange hair rose wildly above his narrow skull, a halo of fire. his skin was amazingly pale to them, his knobby sunburned shoulders inspired a weird awe in them. they knelt in his path as he approached the fire chanting, his legs shifting in a jerky dance as his bare feet encountered numerous sharp obsidian stones along the crushed path. it was the fated return of Lono, the reincarnation of Captain Cook. johnny werd's ribs were clearly visible and the natives who surrounded him were roundshouldered and beautifully muscled, they became prostrate in his wake as he wandered confusedly ashore looking for a pop machine. the storm would return and lash the island with all its terrible fury threatening to reclaim as the seas anything easily disassembled by monsoon winds. as the fire whippped in the rain and ferocious winds, clinging to its tenuous root of flaming wood, they all held johnny aloft as a sacrifice or show of power to the storm god. the wooden idols came alive in the stormstung confusion and horrible vacuum into the pacific abyss, their vaguely geometrical wooden slants frowning in metaphysical disappointment, the storm whipped ecstatically, screaming primal manslaughter oblivion unrolling harsh electrical network whose impacts were drowned by the wet roar. save us johnny werd, they shouted, holding his scrawny body with the third degree sunburn and the bad trunks aloft, save us. johnny's glasses blew off and he began to cry.

werd awoke to the sting of the explosive phone ring. the doctor skwawked through the lines: the diagnosis had arrived: mono nucleosis. poor johnny. in his dream johnny was attacked on the streets of Manhattan the day his record went platinum and although johnny complied with the assailant's gruff request for valuables more rapidly and efficiently than he had ever completed any thought or action, his 15 year old supermodel girlfriend in the red strapless backless bikiniless minisuit refused to hand over her cherry red leather purse, pouting her lipstick in the indignance that had awarded her her entire life a position of power over rich men, the only men she had known.

"GIVE HIM THE MONEY!!!" screamed johnny putting her in an armlock and reaching for her purse which she held as far away from his grasp as she could (being two feet taller in high heels) (him in Keds)

all the companies who own the rights to the products endorsed in this manuscript have paid me gloriously vast sums of money and i am now fabulously wealthy and own several suits.

so johnny got stabbed a hundred times and then the teenage glamour queen beat off the attacker. johnny was bleeding critically from several severe wounds, which was complicating the symptoms of mono nucleosis, which he had. mono nucleosis must be the most demoralizing of the nonfatal diseases by virtue of its persistence. it is to sleep for 24 hours straight occasionally referring to a glass of water by the bedside for advice and consolation.

vultures circled overhead silhouetted against his bedroom ceiling and hearses circled the block. had Mr.werd issued a last will and testament yet? his lawyer whispered into the telephone... the fate of his Sit'N'Spin was in question.

i will get them, johnny decided, i will get them all and he rose heroically from bed and walked a step towards his chemistry table where the elements of his elements lay in glittering piles. should he take the second step? he wasn't sure, waves

of unconsciousness passed between him and the room, his
blinking vision screwed and dilated, tried to readjust to the
new standing altitude and his blood hammered in his ears.
stop that hammering, john muttered. his furious passion for
vengeance now overcome by his divine puniness, his spectacular
weakness in the face of obstacles such as his own tendency to
be overwhelmed by helplessness. was it any use? it was to no
use. no avail, alas, werd trembled between the first and second
steps, undecided, unsure. he reached a trembling scrawny arm
towards the table which made it hard to be funny. and what of
Ed? grasped a testtube which he pulled towards his thin green
lips and spat into it: kiss.

with some adjustment, with some calculations... by adding
ammonia and methane and exposing his saliva to lightning the
mono nucleosis bacteria would evolve into a land animal and
werd would unleash them to roam the country in wild packs.
dangerous storms excited the ocean to a frothing fever pitch of
delirium and threatened to engulf the entire continent. he was
about to have another nightmare. dream, nightmare, in the
orientationfreefreefall of constant exhaustion the distinction
between nightmare and dream was no longer a sensible one.

the heat closed in in billowing orange waves

the surface of the planet X%^6 consisted of layers of shattered
orange tectonic plates and captain werd stumbled from plane
to plane, leaping rents in the earth and sliding treacherously
close to the abyss into the raging green soup that raged beneath
the planet's meteor shattered surface. he had to get back to the
Ship to retrieve his Ray to Blast the Creature that was pursuing
him, bubbling viscous purple fluid, a tentacled acid blob flowed
in his footsteps. which ray shall i choose? he wondered... the
Vaporizer? the Atomizer? he adjusted the gravity using a dial on
his wrist and leapt several stories into the air and using his heel
rocket managed to land comfortably close to the dome. he opened
the dome and grabbed his Ionizer. Zap! the Creature retreated
in scorched humiliation. captain werd grabbed a Space Beer,
drained it. this planet sure was hot. his stripes flashed in the
sun. then the universe imploded.

a lightfortnight away, in the industry-ravaged slums of the second moon of the third planet in the New Alpha system, the pills came on as I exited the alley and the first indication was the intricate neon calligraphy reflected in the beads of water condensing on my red plastic raincoat. one of the replaced croaked for a tab so with an arc of deadly blue I welded him to the plasphalt where his remains bubbled and hissed. Silicon Sally was leaning against the plate glass of the pharmaceutical and recreational sex division trying to score a ride and we smoked cigarettes together in silence. from here we could see the tip of the corporate pyramid, several miles distant, belching the flames of excess oil pressure against the opaque sky. with her blade she removed the panel from her forearm and adjusted her visual acuity, cranking it. now her vision was telescopic and she could see, quite clearly, at the top of the pyramid Head hard at work behind his desk buying and selling things. or playing holochess for all we could tell. he was wearing virtual goggles and gloves and it was impossible to decipher his actions.

we remembered cybernerd JW6, our brother. before he became an astronaut, werd would wander the slums being harassed by gangs of burners or the solitary wheezer on every corner. more than once, his glassses were removed and stepped on, his hair mussed, his plaid shorts pulled down to his bony knees.

# Johnny Werd: the truncated lacerated edited shorted undignified accessible conventional bland ordinary Paris Review sell-out version that will reap me tons of money and a private mansion in the Massachusetts countryside with two dogs named after dead British poets and potted ferns

My belly is ripped open to the universe and the creatures that orbit brilliant stars ingesting rings of orbital dust mingle with the worms who digest my food and my brain is a bucket of water flung into the air and flashfrozen at the apogee of its arc. People drive by roll down their windows and shout things at me pointing. I hide in someone else's basement unable to surrender my anonymity enough to have an address, I am concealed behind someone else's... I cough black flecks in a spatter across cement and occasionally crawl upstairs gnarled and snarfing pastry, grunting through nostrils of cake.

Johnny Werd coughed splinters of teak and balsa and squatted elegantly over a model railroad zipping figure eights while 8 preened and kept stern observation notes. Werd wasn't sure if he was science fiction. His body was fueled constantly by various chemicals until he was too tired to do anything except sleep and his every thought involved sleep & he slept with electrodes plugged into his darkening brain. He would ingest the crystalline meth by mean of a binary electrode code stimulating the overlit mechanical regions of his brain. Werd drove around on his mountainbike his dreams of colliding with an automobile a vague erotic splendor reminiscent of tragic narratives. He rode his bike along the highway without so much as a styrofoam helmet and the cars whizzed by at upwards of 70 MPH spewing doppler-affected curses. Someday one of these cars would hit him and all that would remain of his genetics was the delicate geometry of the fractured hull of the car. The V-shaped indentation in the bonnet and the shattered frosted dust of the windshield and a vague smear of some genetic paste that was once him. And the eroticism of this nightmare lured Werd into some overlit realm of bizarre scientific encrustations. In some vehicle and always compelled by the eroticism of crashes. His chromium pubis intersecting the dashboard in a variety of tangents. This overlit stylized geometry was the manifestation of the perfection of the landscape of the eroticism of the cortex of the main character, Gianni Werd. Weird's fondness for kitchen appliances was the latent erotic realization of some apocrypha etched deep in his shiny cortex. He photographed his blender and crossreferred the enlargements with photos from an old anatomy textbook depicting laceration wounds inflicted by machinery. Late at night he would walk the cat, which zigzag jerked the leash in a ricochet of neurotic tangents shrieking and his intermittent hair fluffed in sick patches. Outside Mrs. Blandale's house a red ambulancelight silently revolved, casting a geometry of red tangents scattered from the reflective surfaces of appliances. Mrs. Blandale was sobbing in a policewoman's arms. Mr. Blandale was being brought out of the house on a stretcher and for a second his damaged hand slipped from beneath the sheet, fingers missing, bandage stained red, before an orderly could slide it again out of sight. All this Werd watched while sipping his own bananamilkshake from a squeezebottle. It was the penultimate erotic moment for Werd, who had never masturbated, and the cat went shrieking up a tree when the ambulance stirred at the curb and the siren let out a warning yelp. At home he stood in the kitchen lit only by a florescent pane and the blue flicker of the microwave clock. He had plugged in the blender and now put his hand in and touched his thumb to the blade, testing its sharpness. He stood that way for a long time savoring the feel of the steel against his finger, imagining the line of the cut. Suddenly his mother called from downstairs:

"Johnnie, are you playing with the blender again?"

"No mother."

He watched Saturday morning cartoons and the sight of the coyote dwindling to a speck, finally a puff of smoke, was the superbly profound solution to his stylized sadotechnomasochistic nightmare. The elaborate contraptions, catapults and cannons, in which the coyote would meet his repetitive demise in uncanny accidents. Occasionally the implied laws of physics were suspended by the team of animators in order for the coyote to meet a more abrupt and surprising end. And what of Sylvester's stilts shortened by the sonically obvious buzzsaws of piranhas and bulldogs. All this Werd watched with bulbous unblinking bloodshot orbs while greedily spooning spoonfuls of frosted oat Whacks to his shiny red maw dribbling a drizzle of milk. The same thing could happen to Dad while working under the jacked up Chevy which had been in the backyard for two years or to Mom assembling a stepladder to reach a secret shelf of the closet. Uncanny accidents. Veins bulged and writhed on Werrd's scalp in a mad dance of hallucinogenic incantations. He went into his L-shaped room, around the corner from the television, and removed from behind a loose brick in the wall his diary. He wrote a postmoderncyberpunkpoliticallycorrect love sonnet:

> We gaze into one another's eyes as floppydiscs are ejected from our foreheads. We exchange them and they disappear into our foreheads which close behind them. Our eyes go blank, blink red as our memories are assimilated. When our eyes come back on they are no longer our own.

He looked through the Whirlpool catalog and cross referenced the appliances with an erotic magazine. This pathway led to some bleak desolate overlit terrain his stylized mind calm carapace crabshell legs extended pincers flailing, a cloud of ink billowing. It was the plateau of his desires.

Werd was now euphoriant, trapped in the insatiable claws of his fondest wish. He had crawled inside the microwave, folded quadruple, and his upsidedownlefthand groped for the controls, set the dial, and attempted to slam the door. He could hear his mother's advancing slippers as the door kept bouncing painfully off his collarbone. The kitchenlights flared on. She had caught him! She strode over to the ajar microwave door and as he watched through the radiationshielded glass she slammed it shut.

"Gaddamned cat!" she spat in fury. Werd could not believe his mom swore even as the first mutations realigned his mental pathways....

*On one of the subsequent days a couple days later*

Still ill, having slept through seven semesters with no apparent effect on his transcript, Werd woke up being handed his college diploma with a red rose and ribbon in the center of an enormous stage by an aging facultymember who provided a warm handshake and a wrinkleeyed smile of nostalgia. Werd was politely escorted offstage and through a rear exit out onto mainstreet in broad daylight. What? No banquet? He couldn't retire on his laurel leaf? He couldn't even spend a year in Europe?

Nope. The real world, baby.

Werd adjusted his mortarboard and scratched his scalp, and proceeded to walk down the street amid traffic and pedestrians in his toolong flowing robes looking for a HELP WANTED sign in a windowfront.

grrr...

Werd got an interview: he was asked to speak before the People's Corporate Power Wedge where chairmen had assembled around an extremely technologically capable coffeetable. They listened attentively, their fingertips together palms separate their fingers the bars of cages in which their boredom was captured. Werd used an overhead projector and the coffeetable had the capability to project holograms of small objects, a dodecagon of holograms, each floating above a different businessman's face. Werd displayed a Starwars figure. The figure was Luke Skywalker in XWing Fighter gear, the helmeted seer. Wwerdd explained to the committee his dreams of becoming Luke Skywalker destroying the existing corporate power structure by inventing a chemical which when mixed with water it would alter the water molecules recombining their inherent atomic parts to create some sort of drug which when added to the world water supply would chemically alter all of the water causing it to become a substance which had every property of water plus one additional property which would cause everyone to die or become blinded or insane (preferably insane) except people who had a bottled water supply (and the means to defend it) or who subsisted on rainwater would become extremely powerful men and Johnny would rank high among them, towering as a prince because he was supplied, he had a plastic 2liter Pepsi bottle of tap water on a high closet shelf where his parents would never find it, and when water evaporated then perhaps hopefully if he was really really lucky then it would become ordinary steam which would recondense as ordinary rainwater so people in severely raindrenched regions would be less freaked out and permanent slaves to the whim of gigantic Megalords like John Werd and the property would descend to the deepest oceanwater which would be the last to be reevaporated and it was difficult to determine the effect on sharks at this point. The chairmen all watched him unblinkingly pretending to be the least bit interested in this inane plot which was after all the plot of this book and the point but Johnny came off as a shattered geek savant with dangerously sociopathic ulteriors because he was old now, on this page, much older now, in his early twenties, his findings had all been published and the radiation was dying down to subtoxic levels in 95 percent of the globe.

Finally they finally finally got him to talk about money: how much the formula would cost.

His formula, the one he had used to reprogram the old world.

### access to the pyramid

> you've got the color
> you've got the grin
> you've got the certificate
> we'll let you in
>
> we've got a stapler
> we've got a desk
> we've got an elevator
> you've got the rest

this aching gnawing anxiety in my balls and lungs won't quit with its tingling. johnny werd slid the coded identity card's magnetic stripe into the slot that was an electronic keyhole and doorknob. with a sigh he slid his briefcase onto the immaculate countertop and stood in the entranceway, warmly lit from a falling sun's glare along the polished oak floor. He loosened his tie with one hand, sliding his grey jacket onto a hangar, pressed the answering machine's button ornamented with the blinking red light emitting diode.*

"Werd? This is Maxwell. We've got a special assignment for you. Tomorrow you'll fly to Hawaii to investigate chemical extracts from coconut milk vis a vis possible use as an insecticide. The war on nature is not yet won. Meet me at the airport at 7AM."

Werd sighed and sank onto one of the leather stools along the bar, reached over, and fixed himself a vermouth & lime. on second thought... he added a little gin and three Spanish olives. He had a lot to think about and he wanted to make damn sure he didn't. In the closet of his spacious bedroom with the vaulted skylight lay his childhood chemistry set and the unsolved problem. His boyhood dreams of selfish global domination had all been abandoned in favor of fast living and the flow of money

that kept his apartment clean. He had transcended his need for
the constant accumulation of toys through simply being able
to afford to buy and throw away any toy he could imagine. He
could have built a yacht with a jungle gym and waterslide, or
ride a donalddduckinnertube up the mighty Nile. He could drink
fabulously exotic soda and candy in exclusive restaurants in
Paris. But at what loss? His parents were very happy with the
widescreen projection television and the satellite dish he had
bought them. At least he assumed they were happy. Yet in the
room above them, the one the fire had consumed, a dream could
not sleep. It thrashed about in Sesame Street bedsheets. Werd
slumped at the bar and ran a hand through his cropped shock of
trim orange hair. Silicon Sally walked in.

Nature does not ask that a bird "earn a living"
quippped Jason misquoting Buckminster Fulller
in a spectacular evasion of the point. He gestured
to the squirrrels, foxes, rabbbits and other
wooodland creatures that had formed a ring
around the campfire, noses twitching at the scent
of the blackened hot dogs we were crunching
betweeen folded sheeets of damp Wonderbread.
I set my halfffinished cigarettte on the rock and
Jason casuallly grabbbed it before I could reach
for the mustard. A doe was inching closer to my
hotdog and I whirled and growled, she retreated.

I don't know... Werd muttered into the phone...
I've never killed anyone before. Not even an insect.
What if... a burst of threatening crackle emerged from the
earpiece urging Werd to reconsider.

Although killing was a sin and illegal and possibly even bad,
Werd reconsidered. With Maxwell out of the way the entire
synthesis and distribution branch of Toxico Unlimited would be
under his control. Maybe the power he had always longed for
was not so far from his grasp after all...

But Werd would have been better off as a painted minstrelman
with toosmall tux creeping above his wrists and tophat & cane
doing a sloppy softshoe on the horribly gaslit stage of this dismal
speakeasy down under where the liquor is fast and the doors
are always locked. The storm outside would lend an otherwise

absent comfort to the glum dampth and cigarette stench.

Werd rolled up some green handgrown prematurely harvested
tobacco and returned to his booth deep in the darkness of the
lounge where Sally stretched a long leg impatiently and watched
him return impatiently lighting an impatient cigarette to
punctuate her impatience. Werd smoked and thought thoughts
to himself thoughtfully. Sally drank her drink until she was
drunk. Sally pursed her lips and rummaged through her purse
pursively. Werd fingered his lapel lapel lapellingly.

> "oh let's DO something." Sally finally insisted.
> "sure doll how about steamy sex?"
> "great! oh you mean with you? well..."
> "badminton?"
> "psshhh."
> "how about squash?"
> "i don't like vegetables."
> "bowling?"
> ""
>
> (stern glare)
>
> Werd put out his cigarette in a blossom of putrid
> green smoke.
>
> "let's roll, doll. i gotta felony to commit."
> "now THAT sounds like fun."

The man with the fedora was obviously a Rev so Werd dropped
a V-spot on the chipped thick wooden table and murmured an
exit to the doorman. As the doorman peered through the sliding
slit, then opened the door johnny werd discovered several
shotguns pointed at his hat. it was a raid. government agents
and wiretappers flooded in and the horrible tinkling piano was
abruptly silenced. he would never get back to West Egg now.

# Analogous Metamorphosing Technique

As every writer knows, a POV transfer can be accomplished by a great many means other than direct contact between characters. For example, I once wrote a story in which Connie Obvious would descend the staircase furtively, afraid of seeing Johnny Werd on one of the floors. On the landing immediately below Maxsh Eeen, she would stop because there was the landing of Ed, and from his door there was a muffled thumping and laughing and the occasional crash of a lamp falling onto the floor would come out from beneath the door underwhich tiny corners of dollarbills would point out. She would walk up to Ed's doorway slowly and the way she would reach out to it slowly was the same way she would reach towards Xteeth, her fingers sliding through his fleshy exterior and Xteeth should wriggle, Y is dislodged and Xteeth collapses into jello on the highway hurtling along towards California or New York which should loom on the horizon at all times. Brian Hagy should stick out his thumb as their convertible hurtles past and off into the distance while he kicks the dust and looks at the purple aardvark, who looks back at tall and thin Brian Hagy. Brian Hagy looks at the purple aardvark with blue spots who is now looking at Maxsh Eeen who wriggles his pincers and spurts sand upwards... Maxsh snaps his claws at Hagy who poses languidly against the glitzy sea and shoots a seductive glance at the purple aardvark with blue spots and red stripes which looks at Maxsh whose stalked eyes now observe Xteeth shooting by on the highway. Xteeth communicates his telepathic empathy with Hagy, sees from Hagy's eyes the growing assembly of ocean creatures and feels Hagy's alienation shifting into fifth feeling alienated from the purple aardvark with blue stripes and red spots. Didn't anyone else see it? It had eyes only for Maxsh who buried himself in liquid sand releasing a final bubble and eyestalks just above the fizzing foam and looking for Xteeth who was gone and empathizing only with Connie... Oh Connie, but you were still thinking about Hagy posed on the beach, resplendent in twenty flannel shirts wrapped around thighs, buttocks, flexing his thorax in front of this anteater which was watching the famous novelist bury himself in sand who had sent Xteeth and her a fleeting glance. But what of Ed whose apartment had filled with dollarbills exploding from the briefcase the government had given him..? Her attention returned to Hagy who posed on the beach for the amusement of the purple aardvark with red and blue plaid and white spots, watching the sand where the crab had sunk...

# I smell Johnny Werd

I was fishing for electrons in the primordial soup using a Johnny Werd lure, tiny with plastic orange hair unraveling attractively underwater like seaweed. I inserted the fishhook into the bridge of his nose and threw him over the lip of the Grand Canyon. After awhile there came a tug as the last surviving member of the Alquauha (a never discovered species of goat able to walk on vertical surfaces due to a special suction created by the hoof) began to chew on Johnny Werd's inflatable basketball shoe—the Hydraulic by Nike—but I lost interest.

120 feet away at a souvenir stand where there was a revolving postcard rack which had hundreds of copies of the same postcard which depicted a 10000 foot high Rhesus Monkey eating a bus filled with terrified Manhattaners all scrambling out the windows lined with broken glass scraping bloody streaks down their sides as a single young man lay in the aisle twitching in the final throes of advanced Chronic Obstructive Pulmonary Disorder clutched as his chest where a pocket with his first name written on it in cursive contained a copy of the very same postcard and below the picture it reads...

I'M EATING LIVE HUMAN FLESH AT THE GRAND CANYON.

These are used postcards. I buy one which is typed. It reads:

Dear Mikey,
Having a lovely time on the corona. Its ten million degrees here and always daylight.
Love Mikey.

So naturally I decided to write a postcard to ex-president George Bush explaining my opinion on war in the Middle East figuring now that since he was out of office he might want to hear my opinion so I put a stamp on it which had a picture of James Joyce's deviated septum with a cutaway view showing the mucosal blockage and mailed it to George Bush's mansion in Massachusetts [where I knew he would be writing his autobiography] by putting it into one of those U.S. Postal

Service vacuum tubes which sucks your letter to its destination anywhere in North America in five seconds and it clicked into a brass tube beside George Bush's desk. George Bush was an inch tall and had to type his autobiography one letter at a time by committing an impressive swandive from the top of his typewriter with a triple somersault.

Let me tell you a little bit about myself. I was Johnny Werd, too. I bit the tip of the tail of the alligator of the destiny of my species and I held on with my teeth as it tried to whip me starward. Death called me long-distance and on the first ring I picked up the phone and bit the mouthpiece off, spat it into my monkey casserole whose steamy entrails and fettuccine noodles were heaped in front of me.

Do not underestimate Johnny Werd. He had the whole thing planned out. First he would build a secret shockproof airtight underground hideout with a lifetime or more of pressurized air. Then he would get a cool haircut. Johnny Werd is typing this right now, halfplunged hypos of speed jabbed in his forearm. He has been typing for 10 days straight. Johnny Werd, ace aircraft mechanic, and pilot, was actually the first American to fly across the Atlantic and land on a runway teeming with French people. He flew with a purple aardvark as a copilot who preened himself ambivalently with his long tongue, gazing out the porthole at foamy breakers. Werd was radioing for help because the altimeter was installed upside down and he thought they were flying at 0005 ft. The aardvark continued his display of nonchalance even while reaching for the radio with his tail to order a pizza. The pizza was misdelivered to President Bill Clinton who sat and ate it with a wide rustic grin of pseudo-proletarian satisfaction. One of the anchovies on the pizza had been imported from Spain where it had been discovered clinging like a leech to the side of Salvador Dali's partially submerged piano. The anchovy was endowed with a particular intelligence, technology bought by the Japanese, designed by Malt—a silicon valley hippy with a Volkswagen bus, a gold coke spoon, and $90,000 a year.

Give up your transparent ideals, Malt, become power hungry! Malt returned to his $1000 a month loft to find that his cat, Juniper, had knocked over his Sinsemilla plants, ravaging the pungent flowers into shreds scattered across the grey wall to wall pile. He stared in amazement as his entire years crop lay clawed and pitiful in a smear of soil across his $2000 carpeting. His normally peaceful bearded countenance grew furious. Enraged, he shrieked: "GOD DAMN YOU JUNIPER!" Juniper was up in the closet with one of Malt's radios: an old wireless army radio whose generator he clumsily tried to crank with his paw. Downstairs he could hear that Malt had grabbed the $100 fireplace poker by Pierre Cardin and was slashing his leather furniture into ribbons, pulverizing his $3500 Hardon-Karmon quadraphonic all-digital stereo console in a slow demolition of the entire flat to culminate in the beheading of Juniper who meowed desperately on every frequency. A crackling voice came back: "This is Tennessee. Is this a distress yowl?" "Meow!" Tennessee leaned over her wireless and said "I'm sorry, there's nothing I can do to help you. I'm in a wheelchair in a trailerhome in the middle of the desert in Nevada. Let me explain my life story, the tale of desperation and despair that led me to this desolate rocky outcropping of hope..." Tennessee explained it all, and eventually stopped to listen to the poor cat-in-trouble's response, hearing only what sounded like a chainsaw ripping through fur coats, or it could have been static... Who knows? Solar flares? Nuclear weapons testing? Say for example that the United States wanted to bomb Nevada, just for old times sake... Boom! Well, best not to think about that too much there, Tennessee. Your hand's shaking. You look startled. Don't you recognize me? You're breathing funny, what's the matter? "Leave me alone you miserable cretin-burger!" Hey now, is that any way to talk to your ex-boyfriend, the Al Capone look-alike? I wanted to surprise you so I came in the back way. Using this: [wields a shiny knife bearing some resemblance to the one Tennessee tried to kill him with ten years ago to the day] But if you're not glad to see me, if you're just gonna yell at me and stuff then—geez—I'm leavin. [exits, walks back to his car] Can you believe the way she acted? Poorly: too unintelligible and overplayed gestures. After all we've been through together and around separately. Who am I talking to anyway? Hey, you, get outta my car! Stinky beat it. Stinky was way out of shape from smoking but no way that old fogey was going to catch him. Jogging raspily down mainstreet, carrying the stolen car radio over his head as if triumphantly to avoid tripping on any of the trailing wires or the rear speaker which bounced along on the pavement behind him, Stinky suddenly realized that he was running down the middle of the street wielding an [obviously] stolen car radio AM/FM stereo

cassette deck with DBX and variable speed. I must be blocking
traffic. I slow to a walk and turn around. A police car is tailing
me closely, the cop [obviously] annoyed. I grin apologetically, reel
in the speaker, step to the sidewalk and get up against the wall,
my hands over my head, and the cop inches on down the block
at 5MPH. "Take me in! I'm guilty!" You inch on down the block,
ignoring the public's pleas for attention, security. Being a cop is
tough, and you can't just bust every punk you see. No. You can't.
You'd never have time for lunch. And this is Friday. Today you're
going to K. H. Knicklebaggy's for a steaming bowl of squid jumbo
with extra turnips on the side. Georgio the waiter always knows
just what you want. You don't even have to order or speak to
him at all. He knows you don't want to talk about the weather.
He's alright—for a young man of ambiguous sexuality obviously
incapable of any real work like defending the streets like you do.
Yep. You're a cop. That's what you do, defend the streets, yep.
You knock the peppermill onto the floor and indicate to Georgio
with an upraised forefinger that you would like another one. He
doesn't catch on that you would like a peppermill. He thinks you
are interested in a relationship. He comes over to your table and
tries to strike up a conversation with you, of all things. Right
there in front of the entire restaurant he says "did you need
something, sir?" "All I wanted was a lousy goddamn peppermill!"
you scream "Not to wake up dazed and euphoric on damp sheets
with the likes of you!" Georgio will appear hurt. He will go
into the kitchen and weep tears into the anchovy broth... "oh
my god! these anchovies are still alive!" Of course we are... We
were designed to remain operable at much higher temperatures
than this broth. We float around in the eddies preparing our
message which goes out through a spatula link in Japanese
binary: "Surrender to the flux of the international market!" The
Manhattan bankers, hearing this beamed directly into their
molars from a soup somewhere they weren't sure what kind,
maybe chowder, drove their limos and hearses off the bridge and
into the murky Hudson. They screamed "WE CAN`T! WE'RE
DOMINANT!" they cried. Sploosh! You all heard them, too. All of
you fled back to the hot volcanic currents shooting out of vents in
the Marianis. They sent another message through the ladlelink:
"ABANDON YOUR CULTURE TO MASS MERCHANDISING!"
At that moment, Antarctica bobbed and rolled over. There
were no casualties. Yet. But Antarctica had come loose from
its moorings and was now floating in the South Pacific, being
gradually nudged up the coast of Chile to the Isthmus of

Panama. Then my keyboard broke, just stopped functioning. So I had to quit Styx. After the dawn of sunset.

A perilous gagged quest Werd hitched himself into the drivers seat and took off...

I come up from the basement
Thumping my ragged callused soles on the
mud cracked steps. Clump. Clump. Thump.
Andy recoils in terror at the overpowering reek,
surrounding me in billows. The perfume of musk oil oxen hooves treading kneading bleating squeaking pining diving tantalizing lips sold with currants, curry, sautéed in a rice soufflé with succotash cacti cream of plaid pterodactyl onion soup mix dijon du jour. The excessive rantings of a dumbo caught between a ukulele slide and naptime crushed by the impotent weight of a bad check, crossed out and no longer made payable to anybody, a fitful doze, a pianolesson tomorrow, my impending merciless retraction period, the subsequent billowing of activity...

"Hey You! Get offfa my cloud!" Me n' Maryanne had parked on a cumulus & apparently it was some guy's space because he was trying to back a pink Cadillac down on top of us. I threw it into reverse causing Maryanne to tumble forwards over the hood and fall through the cloud. "I'll save you!" I yelled. The pastures below, squared off by lines demarcating private ownership, spiraled closer in a sickening acceleration. Johnny was above, driving straight down, twirling. I screamed: "[scream]" He banked left at the last second so my flock wasn't impaled, staggering southwards in a V formation towards Sarasota: our winter nest. My left aileron needed grooming so we began to descend slowly through layers of wispy cirrus. We set down in a beanfield which offered us a tasty treat of beanbeetles scrawling zigzags against green leaves, gulp gulp. I snoozed there for a second, standing up & dreamt of flying through a Hawaiian monsoon...$

*Metanoïa*

--------------------[PANEL]--------------------

# IT WAS A RAINY AFTERNOON, AN AFTERNOON LIKE ANY OTHER...

[ring, ring!!]

emanates from phone on bedside table
seen from overhead tinyman's legs and
boots and the copy of U.S.A. TODAY he
reads. his thoughtcloud reads

[Zzzzzzzzzzzzzzzzzzzzzzzzzzzzzz]

comic book over his face, JW slept through all five alarms. the
first was a dove whose leg was attached by a golden chain to
a silver pail of icewater containing live thrashing trout and at
seven AM the dovecagedoor would automatically open and the
dove would try to fly out the window, the chain tightening and
knocking the pail off its marble pedestal sending icy whipping
fish cascading down across JW's pillow but he didn't wake up. the
second alarm was limited nuclear warfare. the third alarm was a
Led Zeppelin concert. the phone rang. the fourth alarm was the
end of civilization as we know it. the fifth alarm was a clock radio
that didn't work but

it was another tiny morning and the tiny sun rose between
the cracks and bulletholes in JW's tiny window. he glazed
contemptuously across his acres of dingy sheets. he opened
another blue bottle of flies, his seventh since the end of the world
began the night before. there seemed to be a smudge on the wall
so JW put in his glass eyes and put on his eyeglasses. it was
indeed a smudge on the wall. his clock radio was offering him

the music of hank angst and the pank twankies. JW was good
at games. four dimensional phonetic boggle and underwater
braille scrabble were two of his favorites. he also enjoyed zero
gravity twister. he used to be good. that was back when he was
a parttime subhero named tinyman. JW was a subhero for many
panels until he had been sued by someone he once failed to
rescue. that person didn't want to press charges but her lawyer
insisted. the night before the court case that person raised a
forkful of limabeans to her mouth. JW winced and ate a slice
of bread to clear his palate. she drank a glass of water, spilled
it down her chin. JW dabbed at his mouth with a napkin. JW
wondered about her, what she must be like, if they could ever
put this not rescuing thing behind them and be friends... JW
hadn't worn the cape in years.

the phone rang a second time.

he stood up from the breakfast table and stumbled off towards
back into the kitchen. the evening sun slanted orange slats.
a angular silhouette in the widening trapezoid of refrigerator
light. half loaf of bread. half bottle of milk. something dark near
the back. a hand with gold bracelet and ruby nailgloss grasps
a bottle of mineral water. clank and pour of milk by JW in
shadows. clank of replaced milk. trapezoid diminishes. skwawk
of bird.
JW in bed reading ripped and tattered notes to Gravity's
Rainbow. nondescript t shirt. striped pyjama bottoms. black and
white t.v. sound turned down. star trek rerun. cigarette smoke.
JW takes impatient drag eyes fixated on notes. commercials with
fast cuts of smiling faces. television's vertical hold slips, pictures
flip upwards. drag. looks at cigarette. throws it out window.
continues to read for quite some time. distant sirens. ruby
nailpolished fingers obscure the word PYNCHO
door. toilet flushes. door opens. pyjama bottoms emerge and
walk off to the left, pulling door almost shut. click and trapezoid
of light appears across door. a shadow moves across it. sound of
paper being loaded into typewriter.

sunrise through venetian blinds. single bird chirp. sound
of percolation. rubynailed hand with spoon stirs sugar into
coffeecup.

tinyman would only see her three more times in his life. once
when she was falling from a blimp, once when she was in a traffic
jam on the golden gate bridge which was about to demolished
by a gigantic tidal wave during the final California earthquake,
and once when he rescued her from the underground laboratory
of an evil entomologist. she seemed detached and bemused by
his rescuing attempts. maybe this would make tinyman feel that
she never wanted to be rescued in the first place, and the whole
lawsuit was embarrassing to her. but they would never speak. he
would rescue her and she would thank him politely.

once, when JW was seven, she would babysit him. neither of
them would ever remember this. he wrote the poem

### text in the wind

i been squandered for poor
i been poured on the floor

i will dissolve like text in the wind
i will dissolve like text in the mind
i will dissolve like text etched in stone


Werd werked as a freelance middleman. Anytime two
people in a transaction weren't comfortable speaking,
Werd would step in and conduct their transaction on their
behalfs, bargaining with himself for hours, and extract
his fees appropriately. Today, at McDonnacha's, many
customers sat down at the plastic tables and summoned
Werd to go the counter for them. Werd took their order
tableside, wrote it all down, and went up to the shiny steel

and spoke clearly: "my client would like a Chimichanga de Jour with extra Sauerkraut." The other day he had acted as U.N. translator. Later he would find any administrative position in any bureaucracy and work for decades until suddenly one day he would have an idea.

Not.

The phone rang a third time. It was exactly 5:07 and Johnny Werd sauntered up the steps whistling, home from his good weekjob of categorizing sound effects CDs. By 5:08 he had loosened his tie and by 5:09 had poured himself into a stiff chair. His whistling reached the frenzied crescendo of "Love Love Me Do Ron Ron." By 5:10 he was finished and pushed the answering machine button. This was his routine. It was always the same message: a computerized voice offering him free food.

His life was in fascinating order, spectacular, precise, everything perfect: a tessellation of consistency. The day was divided into eight three hour long trours. Three of those were spent at work and lunch. The next three were spent making sure the other twelve were perfect.

So, he winked on his mainframe and as the Granny Smith clucked into proper working order, Werd tightened his own resolution with a screwdriver. The screen fizzled into existence briefly displaying all information, and then a cute animal in 57 colors and a perfect amicable human voice synthesis said "Hello, User!" He had a directory entitled Core. Inside that were folders called Hub, Axis, and Foci. He clicked on Hub and it opened to reveal a rectangle labeled Nucleolus. He hit return. The computer chirped "How are you feeling today?" and would not proceed until he clicked on *O.K.* thirtynine times. Then he opened the file called Perimeter. This was where his organizational plan was meticulously laid out carefully like deliberateness. This was a private file and everyone in the city had access to JW's and everybody else's.

There was a subfile called Here Now and it contained a list of scheduled activities for the rest of Werd's projected life as well as an accurate representation of his finances for the next five decades. It was till 5:10 and under 4 October 1994 5:10 was written "reading this." At 5:11 he was to "compile all birthdays into a separate file called birthday and then activate the Time Condenser software to schedule an hour for every birthday he considered relevant, rescheduling all other activities accordingly, subtracting time from sleep when necessary. Then the cat fell off the refrigerator and unplugged the computer and it crashed, leaving a smoking hole in the tabletop and one in the floor beneath.

Then the phone rang a fourth time.

"Hello?"

"Werd?"

"Yes, this is Mr. Werd. To whom am I speaking?"

"Listen kid... it's Enslin's birthday."

[dramatic organ swell]

Werd shrieked in dismay rending apart sky and earth and steel reinforced concrete sending a shower of splintered soul straight into the malignant eye of the sun whose sickening crimson tinge winced and glass shattered plastic melted sand scattered clothing tattered Werd stumbled out onto the balcony screaming and pounding the balustrade with his mighty fist, hammered down a glinting smooth gnarled clot of marble cascading sparks until the railing itself was a twisted catastrophe.

Then he felt better of course and stood and gazed across the city with its silent pneumatic elevated transport and communal agricultural area, the recording studios and Sound Effects warehouses, the amphitheater in the very center of the city where the open mike was each night when the week's farmers returned from the outlying ginger and onion fields and the week's musicians had almost finished their harmonic system. It was only Tuesday so they had only been in their positions since the time of the Burrito. It was the sixth Burritoweek of the new world (6 B.)and the ninety percent who were unemployed that week were writing theatre for the radioshow busily on secret computerfiles that everyone had access to.

It began to rain. These were the sort of gentle inquisitive raindrop that almost falls on your head but veers back up into the sky at the last moment.

So... this was Enslin's birthday. How was he to find Enslin in time? They were all allowed to choose a new identity and profession every week and Werd had become a jerk and lost all his friends just two weeks hence. Er, I mean prior. Perhaps some of his experiments were producing results worthy of Enslin's birthday. For example he had started a culture culture in a petri dish but it didn't look like it was going to have spoken Sound Effects anytime soon. Perhaps a book... But Enslin already had it, whatever it was, and he already needed to keep all his books in a different house.

Three Burritos ago, when Werd and Enslin had designed and implemented the system of aqueducts which delivered a constant stream of warm bananascented bubblebathwater to every tub in the city, Enslin had confessed to Werd of a desire to study the tapes of Sound Effects the city had accumulated.

You see, Enslin said to Johnny Werd as he poured a test bottle of purple shampoo into the wooden trough and adjusted the incline with his compass, the Sound Effects began as recordings left over from the years B.B. However, to our ears, none of those sound effects sounded real. The buses sounded like dragons, the kitchen appliances sounded like earthquakes, the dreams sounded like nightmares. It was then that we began to tape our own Effects and add them to the collection. Some of them are not what they sound like. The whale is actually a lion, because a lion sounds more like a whale than a whale does. Of course, this

library is continually growing, but is continually being reused as well. We all recognize the lion as the whale: there is no question that the sound of the lion signifies the whale. The sound of the lion has become the whale's key signifier. The sound of the lion is more indicative of the whale than the sound of the whale, the photograph of the whale, the cartoon of the whale. The whale itself is virtually unrecognizable. It sounds funny, what do you think it is? Pass me that towel, I'm going to try taking a bath now.

So Enslin, a day before the Burrito on which he changed his name, explained to me that the language of the Sound Effects was more significant that the one we speak. He wanted to make a radio play with incorrect sound effects, or correct sound effects which occurred in the wrong order, or opposite order. Mark, I told him now serious now my face raven graven with solemn intent, you can't do that. It might upset the Burrito.

To this he issued a squeak, signifying rubber duck, in response.

Werd wasn't sure is he was in a flashback anymore or what. And what was that part about the restaurant? What the hell, was he at his computer or ricocheting down the turquoise shampoo lubricated aqueduct angling towards a private bathtub which everybody in the city had access to. And if he wasn't in the flashback, then where and who were these Enslin fellas anyway? Hmmm... Maybe Werd could figure it out...

Enslin, Enslin. Hmmm... Mark Enslin. I'm Irk Insulin. Omar K. Nasaline. Um... Enarm Slink. Enlink Mars. R.E. Kilnsman. Lime'n'Snark. Snarem' Link. Um... Reek An Isle On? Amerikan Slain! Mire Kin Sail In. Murky Noose Lion. Mime Error Kansas Lily Neon. Murmur Kan-Kan Salsa'll Lull Lanolin. Um... Nile Seek Roam. Analyse Ink Arm. Nul Sunk Rum. Nails Ankor Mom. Nine Loyal Assesses Nono Kook Rarer Maim.

Werd wobbled and almost fell off the balcony into the intricate scaffolding below. Splash! In pseudopods of aquamarine foam JW slid off the edge of the duct and landed in Enslin's bathtub sinking many boats.

Or was it?

Something has gone wrong in the maturation process.

Werd has rats in his head. They keep you awake. They are within the walls, scrabbling. They chewed through the wiring and made your computer short out. You try to sleep and you hear them behind your head, squeaking. What you thought was an attic was a skull. You've been living here two years, finally you decide to take a crowbar to the drywall. There are skeletons back there, but you keep ripping the panels to dust, popping nails, until you find the twin windows that have been covered over: Werd's eyes. You pull the walls away from the inside of Werd's eyes but the panes have been painted white. You take a chisel and scrape a gash in the white of Werd's eyes so you can see out.

You cup your hand over the window and see out.

You don't like what you see.

after too many extraneous digressions, johnny werd was by now an adult who automatically capitaliZed the first letter of every sentence. in the natural progression from childhood to global domination to college to temp work, werd had abandoned chemistry in favor of safer vocations. he rode the streetcar to work his pale countenance glazed with indifference. occasionally he might have a muscle spasm but that was as expressive as he got. the subway hurtled through oblivion and werd paged through the sports section. he still was not interested in sports but the counseling he was undergoing had shown some signs of success. now he read the sports section first and

then he went to the story about the explosion at
the factory. he had known this article was in the
paper and now he was going to read it. he started
to get all excited and fought off another muscle
spasm. he read with fascination that part about
the severed hand. then there was a photograph
of a dead ethnic albanian. he searched the face
for some sign of death, some flavor or color, some
sign of decay. he had a violent muscle spasm and
his head bit the back of the seat. on the front
page of the *tribune* was a graph showing the
shocking extent of American sexual dysfunction.
a huge percentage of people reported that they
were not interested in their partners and this
was interfering with their sex lives. in a scientific
study sponsored by viagra. johnny werd started
to imagine being married to someone he did
not like and imagined himself unable to get an
erection. the thought was terribly arousing and
he started to get an erection but had another
muscle spasm and flopped into the aisle, the
*tribune* scattering under the seats of the airplane,
which banked to the west, the sun golden behind
a layer of smaze. his doctor had told him to read
only sports, his fetish for bad news was really
unhealthy. back in his seat in the back of the bus
he picked up the TWA in-flight magazine. inside
was an article about striking TWA workers. a
bead of spittle formed beneath johnny werd's
lower lip and descended like a spider into his lap.

a cough split the silence like too many machine guns
rattling off an epidemic understatement or dismantling the
military. johnny werd felt the bayonet go in just above his kidney
in a warm spurt of blood.

# Temping at Echelon

Johnny Werd stole a lot of copies the summer he temped at
Echelon and hoped he didn't get caught, hoped nobody was
monitoring the copymachines access codes, tracking copies.
He always had such fantasies though. The paranoia kept him
awake. He would use the company computer to search for the
most subversive websites he could. His group supervisor Linda
Thompson probably wouldn't have cared. There were spooks
in and out of the office at all times, always someone acting
suspiciously, a stranger in a suit with a wire in his ear, military
haircuts. FBI CIA NSA IRS ATF BATF DOD, Werd didn't
know or care. These odd men of the Echelon taskforce, living
vicariously through the lives of more interesting men, living at
the shadowy intersection of the extreme potentials of law and
technology. Those they spied on practiced the arts of terrorism,
insurrection, revolution, espionage. Moving without detection
or fear, remaining invisible, shadows moving through the grid.
Werd hated it there. He sometimes brought drugs, guns, or
bombs to work, just for the kick. Once he brought in an AK47
assault rifle in a dufflebag, kept it in his cubicle, and looked
his boss directly in the eye when she stood before his desk and
handed him copies of the Posse Comitatus Act, the Bill of Rights
and the Constitution and requested that 1000 copies be sent
out to all employees. Werd pinned a photo of Malcolm X over his
telephone. Working there he had seen pass through the office
at various times Oliver North, George Bush, Bill and Hillary
Clinton, Al Gore, even, once, he was sure, Vince Foster. Once,
when retrieving some files from the S cabinet he found files
labeled SPECIAL FORCES, SPECIAL OPERATIONS, SPECIAL
OPS... Sometimes he used the phone to play prank calls on
strangers drawn at random from the phonebook or from the
NASA directory, and he would babble on and on to them about
Ruby Ridge and David Koresh of the Branch-Davidians who died
in the standoff at Waco, Texas a year before the Oklahoma City

bombing , or the Whitewater Scandal and its relation to Iran-Contra. The voices he ranted at over the phone were variously upset or interested or bemused, but none of them found any of it the least bit credible.

At the end of the summer he would be fired for making unauthorized photocopies.

It was a day like any other.

If Johnny Werd had just gotten off of work and was heading for the soft chair in his apartment, the adjective *soft* would have been used to tell *which* chair. Johnny Werd had never felt like this, his skull like some aluminum cantaloupe rind buckling with the pressure from within. If Johnny Werd is in fact a vampire he eats blood and therefore there must be food curdling in his veins and then perhaps this stake which I have poised over his terrified heart is perhaps one of those toothpicks with colored curly cellophane or an American flag. I would be the mysterious character in the attic, pulling the various episodes of Werd's life together into a smooth and compact novel, like life, a smooth texture of parallel meanings, nutshellesque, slithy. All would be perfect nonsense but to them but, above their ceiling, the tapping of the keys, the infernal keys, would signify organization. Even jusybdkll jsus ddom kssi would sound profound when they could only hear the typing, through the ceiling as they watched TV from the ornate clutter of the living room and consequent television. Dad rattled his paper and squeezed off a harsh sigh.

It was too much for Werd, all the job required was the paperwork, not his presence and his code and theirs blended, mingled, forming giant telepathic networks, but in the office merely the hum of the fluorescents, hum of the CPU, hum of the airconditioner, hum of conversation, the hum he hears all the time now anyway and somewhere the hum of indiscernible muzak. He has half an hour for lunch and walks two blocks to the reassuring consistency of the corner grocery and purchases exactly one half pint of milk. During these halfhour intervals he has first learned how to make them last a halfhour. He sits in the park watches pheasants and grouse and thinks that only the freest people are not aware of their restrictions, limitations, and daily backaches. He thinks it has to do with the senses. He glances at his watch. He drains the other half pint, tosses the carton exactly aside into the garbagecan. He is on his feet and halfway back to work before he realizes it. He walks back through the multiple fluorescents and hums and sits down at his desk. He remembers that one of his coworkers is taking physical therapy lessons to learn how to sit down at a desk properly. The lessons are very expensive. He laughs about this as his daily backache rips through his spine.

As the sun screws itself out he imagines staying here in the office until dawn and the fantasy sends a tingling of pleasure deep into his lower back. He imagines the abrupt cessation of several hums as most of the building's systems are shut off at seven and can feel cold swirls of purple night caressing him through an open window. He knows there are some games on this machine. He could make an entire pot of coffee and just sit up, listening to the radio, exploring the computer, clicking on unfamiliar icons, listen to the radio. He would learn to sit down properly, he resolved, and left.

Werd, Werd, the violinist in the corner of the candlelit hotel restaurant seemed to sing, wherefore artthou ... Werd was alone now, the writer had been taken away by his entourage. Werd sighed and the crimson rose seemed also to sigh and droop on its long stem in the hotel restaurant vase. The shadows flickered, as shadows will when cast by candlelight.

Werd, Werd.

The shadows were long and deep and lovely. The night was cool and outside and Werd was inside, inside, unlike the weather which was outside, and Werd was inside, where the airconditioning and candlelight was. And the writer was somewhere else, upstairs perhaps, perhaps in the bus, guarded by those men, those strange men with the tailored suits and dark glasses who tapped on their computers late at night.

upstairsperhaps

And the bartender sighed and Werd hadn't realized the bar was there or that he was there and decided to pay and leave, to walk out into the night and the weather and the city and to think about things. And so did.

A moon sawed through the underbelly of night, its sickle like the cutlass of a pirate, slicing through the black belly of a whale.

Werd walked past the Alamo and into the wreckage of hotels and pavement immediately beyond. Cars drove by with people who made him nervous. Thus he attempted to circumnavigate and return to the hotel but instead found his way on the wrong side of the Alamo and ended up back in the riverwalk district. Cops on bicycles gathered and discussed matters and eyed Werd as he stepped off the curb to bypass them, hands thrust in jacket pockets and tie flapping. Eyes down or straight ahead, trying to follow the meandering path of the river below on the city sidewalks above.

This is the way of things, he thought, and that was all he was able to think.

Simon the secretary glanced up at Johnny Werd as he appeared in the doorway. He was kind of tall and handsome behind his spectacles. His red hair rose in a smooth pompadour, like a gleaming fender. His cotton suit hung from his tall frame, slouched in the doorway.

The secretary asked "do you like jazz?"

Werd had been at this company for a few weeks and he knew from painful experience not to let Simon back him into a corner first thing in the morning.

Werd blinked and came back at him like a cornered badger:

"Well what kind of jazz are we talking here? There's all kind of jazz. Solo vocal combo, Big band, be-bop acidjazz, forites fifties sixties seventies eighties nineties, we got in jazz out jazz and way out jazz. And you got your standards. I mean, can you clarify the question? Otherwise I don't think I can answer it. Sorry."

Werd walked swiftly through the lobby, waving away Simon's response, and passed safely into the interior of the building. He blinked and caught his breath and thought the word "coffee" and looked down a very long corridor. At the end of the corridor the Administrator passed nervously across the hall from one room into another. Even at this great distance it was obvious from the intensity of her velocity that the Administrator was extremely nervous about something. In that instant and at that distance the Administrator was fractal, every movement swift and inefficient, crawling with anxiety, all over the map, scattershot, creating effectiveness through overextended effort. Adrenaline with a smattering of accuracy.

Werd moved quickly up the corridor and turned left at the door into the coffeeroom.

It was bad, it left a pitiful taste, as if a mouse had crawled into one's mouth and died, and eventually an aching dehydrated hollow constricted pain in the chest, and he drank it out of styrofoam, which was nonbiodegradable and which released ozone-destroying Chloroflorocarbons into the atmosphere. And he needed it worse than a blind newborn kitten needed a teat, and his groping was just as inept but persistent.

Coffee. Very good. Yes.

Time, then, to confront the Administrator and prepare the training tapes for the new Carbide chemists who were being reassigned to the Ziploc assembly line.

Then to the boardroom and the meeting with the confused technicians who had had trouble with their English ever since mastering Java. Then onto the Powerpoint presentation in the cafeteria. After that perhaps a twenty-minute exodus for lunch, to eat a hot dog standing up on a busy sidewalk. And then there would be a reprieve for the checking of the email, which would likely flower into a magnificent bloom of additional work.

And then, and then...


"Johnny, come into the breakroom, it's Agnes' birthday. We're having a little lunch. I made Sloppy Joes."

Johnny Werd stared up at the secretary and stammered, his mind unable to fix upon an excuse. He had been lost in concentration, staring at the Dow Janitorial Training Manual, trying to decipher an informational diagram which, through several illustrations with circles and arrows, demonstrated how to wring out a mop. Werd's face went blank and pale, his mouth open, looking up at the secretary who looked down at him steadily.

He swallowed. "Be right there." And he managed a weak smile as a sort of punctuation.

In the break room the atmosphere was festive but limp, like a wet piñata.

Werd spooned a scoop of wet meat onto a white bun on a paperplate. He sat in a corner. Gladys referred to him as "the token male" with an edge almost of malice. Werd smiled emptily. Chatter perpetuated. A photograph of newborn baby was passed around. They laughed at his reaction. Like a man's.

Werd, eviscerated, stumbled down the corridor to his office. On the way he thought about the News, and the Dupont bombing. He wondered whether the air was safe.

He remembered a chemistry experiment he had attempted as a child. That childhood world he had destroyed himself with a pale indelible flame while experimenting.

Werd entered his office and, unable to sit, looked out the window. He saw a tree with slender branches bending under the weight of a squirrel.

He moved closer to the window.

Two floors beneath him, a babycarriage rolled along the crowded sidewalk unaccompanied.

Werd's breath seized and his heart screamed. He blinked hard and challenged reality. *Am I seeing things?* He looked up the street the direction the carriage had come from. He saw a woman struggling with a man. He looked downhill, and saw the hill get steeper. The carriage moved between people, people in hats and raincoats with shoppingbags, some of them stepping aside to avoid it.

As Werd sprinted out the door of his office, his pencil fell onto the training manual, rolled down one of the pages, across the table, off the edge of the table, and fell, turning about 90 degrees of arc to stick point-down in the orange carpet.

Werd burst out the fire exit onto the crowded streetlevel. He had lost his perspective and could no longer see the carriage. He took two steps in the direction his instincts screamed that he should go in. And stopped, staring helplessly into the indifferent train of passersby.

Then he walked the other way .

The cruelty of the times always astonished Johnny Werd. Through his second gin and tonic he might cast a gaze up at the parrots in the cage over the bar and say "The cruelty of the 20th Century is too much for a sane mind to fathom, so it's hard to blame people who don't seem to care."

Having said this he might solemnly suck the cocktail onion off the end of the yellow plastic sword, or maybe there would be the sigh of a match and the lighting of another menthol cigarette. He might gesture, sweeping his arm, palm upturned, across the front of the *Wall Street Tribune* as it lay draped across a barstool, as if it said it all. And perhaps for Werd it did.

But the topic of the times would now be closed for the remainder of the evening. Eventually, even the bar would close, but until then Werd would think only about work. Werd worked developing training programs for corporations. He worked mostly on the production of videos. When working for a client, he would spend weeks on site, so he traveled frequently. This month he was in Midland where he commuted in a daily cycle between a room at the Velour Hotel, the corporate headquarters of Dow, and the bar.

Another, he waves.

The bartender understands that Werd will be ordering a different drink each time. And he understands that this scrawny man with the wiry red hair and the round spectacles will be difficult and attempt to throw him for a loop. This time it will be absinthe or an Income Tax Cocktail. The bartender walks off, unaffected, to search for vermouth and bitters. Werd is struck, now, with an idea for a video he's working on, that instructs Dow Managers on how to fire newly-bought employees.

Werd pulls out a pen and reaches for a cocktail napkin:

> Scene. Long shot. Fisheye, A long long corridor.
> At the end of the corridor is a tiny person in an office chair, perhaps 100 meters off. The person speaks and is clearly audible: "Perkins... you're fired."
>
> Outside shot, camera points up, at the base of a building. Perhaps 200 meters up glass moves outward glittering from the path of an office chair being flung through the window. A man in a suit appears, tumbling head over heels straight at the camera.
>
> Lens cracks. Blackout.

Satisfied, Werd drains his income tax cocktail and gestures for a Jaegermeister. He proceeds to tell the bartender a long answer to a question the bartender has not asked.

"What am I doing with my life Johnny? I mean I'm gonna be thirty in a month, I got nothing to show but a lousy job, and a closetful of manuscripts. I got everything I need to buckle down, I mean really buckle down, plan out the next ten years, make lists and execute them ya know. I mean, jeez, this hotel room I got—top floor, no AC—hotter than hell up there Johnny.

I gotta focus. I can't focus. The heat and this damn numbing job. You ever worked for a transnational Johnny? They fly you places. At first it seems romantic. At first. Helping secure capital and all. Then you look back at who you were but the door's locked. There's bars on the window. You expand your credit, get fat, and then you can't move anymore. You gather moss and investments and assets and you buy things, they get more expensive and less fun, tossing off cash. It's like falling in love too many times, Johnny, you ever fallen in love too many times?

I gotta figure out a way out, Johnny, I gotta get back. But I can't get back.

It's gonna be Y2K soon, everything's gonna change. You ever think about- huh? Yeah, I'll take another, gimme a, uh..., can you mix me an International Incident Johnny. It's in the book. Yeah. Thanks. Y2K. everything's gonna change. Just like I'm sitting here at this bar in this big highrise, and there's neon on the glass and a cyberjuice espresso bar downstairs, but I might as well be sitting here in a fedora, and this might as well be like, an art-deco joint from Berlin in the 30's. You see? This is going to be old-fashioned. And quaint. And next year I'm going to be an anachronistic 30-year-old moving like an ashen ghost through a transformed world. A world of hyperviolent Woodstock concerts and full-scale military assaults against obscure countries that aren't our enemy. A world of killing and fabulous computers. There's a noose tightening around the population—the wealth gap—it's a razorwire garrote that's going to sever us into two species, and those two species are going to be at war. But not for extermination or submission or acquisition. It will be a war of domination. A few frail giants will walk across the hardened shells of the rest of us, and we'll be crunching like cockroach exoskeletons underfoot. We're going back to slavery, and it's going to have a brand new name.

Outsourcing.

Prison labor.

Global economy.

Expansion of capital.

War, slavery, ignorance.

Not:

Strength, peace, freedom.

Ever read Orwell, Johnny? Ever read Marx? It's one of those crazy things. Like a particular form of insanity: sanity. I pick up a bottle like this, see, oh, hey, sorry guy I wasn't trying to take your beer I was just demonstrating, so I pick up, uh, an empty bottle over here and I see clearly the fingerprints. I see the people slaving in the heat of the brewery, their union busted. I see their children's scars. I see migrant workers moving across a field of hops while pesticide rains from above. I see minimum wage and less.

I tell you: you read that shit and it wrecks you. Like a virus of the mind. Like God or truth. I don't have a family Johnny. Because, well, mostly because nobody loves me, but also because I see the family as a fiction. The family is supposed to take care of you and teach you morality so that the state doesn't have to provide for those who can't make it. I get so lonely sometimes Johnny in that hotel room that I'll program three movies in a row. I was watching David Lynch, Quentin Tarantino, some Coen brothers. Natural-Born Killers, Silence of the Lambs. Hyperviolent art movies of the nineties. A new theatrical experience freed of good guys, if you get me. A world without redemption or heroes or love, just killers who fascinate and mesmerize us in their unflinching viciousness. What a sick fucking country this is. This is our art, and it doesn't resemble art. Oh sure, it's beautiful and hypnotic but it has no flesh—it has scales, it isn't human. There are no motivations that would lead to an improved world, nothing sustainable.

I used to think maybe I was an asshole, or clinically depressed, or maniacally introverted, because I hated parties and would rather stay home. Write novels to put in a drawer. Parties, with their suspended motivation. Like a psychological vacuum, an ether, in which one drifts into the bliss of a moderate amount of alcohol. Like a swimmingpool on a hot day, you go in and are refreshed by the clarity of the cool water, glittering and amniotic, relaxed by the exertion required for slow movement. And you don't think about... books... or computers... while you're in there, Johnny, because that shit ain't waterproof. And you're in the pool with a lot of people, maybe total strangers, and you're all almost naked and wet, and it isn't awkward at all. it's comfortable. Very comfortable.

I like swimming, Johnny, but I like to swim laps, swim underwater, go off the diving board. I like to swim in a direction.

What... Brad. Right. Brad not Johnny. Johnny is my name. Sorry Brad. Man, how embarrassing. Well, I guess you must get a lot of people in here forgetting your name. Oh. Not really, huh. Well.

Well, I read this book the other day and now I know. I don't have a good time at parties. and it's not because I'm an asshole- what?

Well, maybe I am an asshole, that's not my point, my point-

Asshole, yeah.

Why you want to go and say a thing like that Brad? Asshole. Fine. Get me another Sino-Soviet Split it's in the book. Jeez. Make yourself useful, seeing as how you aren't going to listen my troubles. Where'd you learn to tend bar anyway? Correspondence course... Asshole...

Why had the bartender called him an asshole?

One hand loosening his bowtie, Werd sat in the darkening room and stared out into the indigo evening, watching lamps come on in the park, on the street, and in the other buildings. He had another cigarette and slid the window open, permitting a cool breeze. The evening had opened up to him. The sky was pure and cloudless. There was a moon.

The phone rang. He let the machine get it. The machine was turned down so he couldn't hear who it was. The machine stopped taking the message and rewound itself.

Time stumbled down the street fifteen floors down taking occasional sips from a brown paper bag.


What was it about Werd that might offer us a clue? In his hotel room, where he sleeps in the chair, cigarette butt extending in a skeletal finger of ash from between his fingers, there is little that will tell us who he his. There is a briefcase. Inside it is all corporate bullshit that makes no sense to us. And there is no nostalgia there, the briefcase may well have been mass-produced, with the contents in it. Let's move on to the suitcase. A number of identical blue suits, shirts, ties, socks, and the underwear. Paisley boxers. Well that at least is a sign of something. Yes. Aside from that, the only other clues to Werd in this hotel room are that the last channel he watched on TV was Cinemax, and the only part of the *Bible* he has read is the word "Bible" embossed gold on the green cover.

There is no Werd here.

He is dreaming but even his dreams, like his salary, could have been predicted by someone who knew the time and place of his birth.

Johnny Werd wore two earrings in his left lobe. His orange hair was shorn into fuzz around his nape and jagged bangs fell in his dreamy green eyes. His tattoo was a skull with thick glasses, broken bridge secured with a wad of masking tape, and he smoked while he did curls, his forearms rippling through the exertion, the strobes catching the beads of sweat refracting reversed images of his apartment over the garage.

Vigi wrote poems on an apple Macintosh and occasionally glancing at the doorway where the skinny silhouette of Werd would assert itself, gaunt and deathridden, the constant angularity of his lines in constant motion. Tonight however she expected to see only the arrival of Dave Zach "wax plumbing foot" Jake, Esquire, an extraordinarily gifted poet from Akron but instead the banging was Werd, thin shoulders spanned against a halfsecond of arc of the Cleveland night. Werd stumbled in and demanded sex. Vigi was afraid of Werd when he was like this: fucked up, sullen, demanding. He went ahead and had sex but her poetic mood was shattered into shards shining shrapnel embedded into various walls which would reflect 12,000 simultaneous images of Dave when he appeared in the ajar door as Werd shook in spasms of fornication sprawled in the corner. Now, seize the moment Dave, clash horns with Werd on a mountaintop! Dave's feathers were ruffled, the feathers on his boa, a rare crossbreed of serpent and chicken, which slithered around his throat where the bowtie was clipped. His manuscripts flickered in the wind.

The poems that Vigi had begun began like this:

### my ragged stumps of syntax

i cannot hit the subject running
the way you do
it stands in my way and confuses me
the way you do

i cannot bounce over the predicate
the way you do
it ruins my momentum
the way you do

Werd stood up, lit a cigarette and refastened his belt quite
smoothly. He lit a cigarette, lit a cigarette, and took a long drag
so intense that the burning point of the cigarette lit the entire
room in blazing clarity of crazy kilolumens and the heat pouring
off of it was so intense that the manuscripts were all incinerated
into dust. Dave tried to think of an excuse to leave. Werd then
extinguishes the cigarette on his own forehead and eats it. "Hey
hows about the three of us going out to a Rave," Werd suggests.
Dave faints in the doorway and Vigi feels trapped between
her desire to receive attention intermittent with narcissism
from two men who can't ever possibly stand one another, both
ultracompetitive in entirely different arenas...

Werd had sex again so Vigi had time to write the next chapter...

That night the thunder lashed fiery vengeance across
the sky and men, for the first time in twelve centuries,
huddled together for warmth... The oppressive fear they
felt had reduced their economic differences to an obscure
fluke of a forgotten game. Somewhere the women had
consolidated on a mountaintop above the angry clouds
and armed themselves and mothernature rained a
vicious wrath, erasing the monuments of industry in
earthquakes, grinding up factories in massive stone

tectonic teeth, rinsing the radioactive waste disposal sites into the ocean where all could be dissolved and recombined to recreate life...

Dave had awoken and now tapped her on her shoulder. He complimented her writing and demanded sex eloquently. He admired the boldly feminist slant of the paragraph whose completion he had interrupted and demanded sex. He drooled a long syrupy soliloquy about the way he admired her when she typed, her gentle fingers stroking the manmade artificial Macintosh keys, her hair bound in a bind that could be unbound thereby allowing her beautiful hair to fall in her eyes, her spectacles which could be removed, her warm sweater cough cough ack. "I'm already having sex with my boyfriend Johnny" she explained, referring to Werd's screams from the corner as he kicked a hole in the wall in orgasmic bliss. That usually deterred all but the few most deluded by grandeur, including Dave. "Welll..." She offered most of her body, but felt that her head and arms should remain typing. Dave drooled another impassioned description demanding her face, or at least an expression of rapture. "Wellll...." She offered everything except a mind and one eye and both hands. Dave drooled a description of her hands describing possible uses for it and "Oh welllll....." Her brain, which Dave did not object to losing, hung before her Macintosh, torn from its skull, joined by bloody nerves to a single eye which hung unblinking before her chapter, joined by a rudimentary connection of ligaments to a skeletal arm wrapped in musculature, fed blood by stretched arteries from her heart which beated in simulated passion beneath a deflated face feigning ecstasy. She found it hard to concentrate on her writing but at least the screams of her two lovers were heard by ears in the adjoining room from her mind... She tried to write but her heart just wasn't in it.

The men, during a calm moment, crawled drenched and sheepish from the niche in the rocks in which they had huddled, and hung their heads beneath an inflamed and furious moon, pulsing red reflecting the fourchambered sun which beat hemoglobin rich blood throughout the world on a system of solar arteries... They had no idea how to refer to the women in their former lives and skirted the subject whenever it came up. Somehow the language of sexual dominance and domestic strife seemed poisonous although they had never discussed it. The memory of their friend Lester being struck by lightning spent from a cloudless sky in the middle of his description of delicious sex with his sixteen year old wife who only two weeks ago had gouged out his eye with a scalding fireplace poker shortly before disappearing along with his handgun and ammo...

Vigi felt a tug on her arteries and realized she was now cooking breakfast for her lovers... Werd had kicked out all the walls and still hadn't come yet, whirls of Cleveland snow drifted in in poetic whorls and whirls and swirls and curls and furls. She was having a hard time continuing her writing even though the scents of her own cooking entered her nose in the next room...

Werd would take her to a rave that night. Dave would stand around in the flickering clicking and drink Happy Sunshine C. Where could her story go from here?

*V.*

The sight of my loins hanging in the butcher's window inspires a deep breath. Another. The hoses clamped to my respirator hisses steam through its slats in the corner. Vapor spews out in torrents of blood gushing through my entrails laid out on the chopping block trailing through the woods to the butchers shop with spires majestic, bleak, fogshrouded and gothic rockers let their hair dangle in the mist from the dry ice smoke machine which billows around the expensive piano, carved from fine hickory dickory dock.

## Q & A

Q: Wait. What happened? I thought the world burned down.

Then allofasudden the Werd kid is going to college and getting jobs? Isn't this equivocation?

A: No. Equivocation is far subtler. What the author is driving at here is a deeper disingenuity. Werd's chemical transformation caused his material and social worlds to waver, shimmer, reveal themselves as language, their construction laid bare with its cruelly arbitrary mechanics. As a result he didn't do well in college and was forced to find work. The world's destruction did not destroy the world, only its meaning. We hold that when something is rendered meaningless, it is destroyed, even if you still have to punch in to it every weekday. Werd's tragedy is all the more tragic in its absence of drama. Werd is a gifted prodigy, abused by his peers, who becomes lost in the obsessions of his own capacity for thought. Genius begets insanity, and in this case insanity appears on the surface to be simple maladjustment or lack of ability. So, Werd lives his life a failure, a temp worker, a raver. And he kills himself in a clumsy and artless fashion while at a particular low point in his erratic employment history.

And how many of us, really, truly make it. To live ones dreams and survive them is rare. Werd is no hero, and this is no novel. Not really.

You asked.

And what of the character in the attic, never mind their plant? They had neither genius nor madness, just a detachment that lent itself to observation. As it turns out, that character is Johnny Werd. Werd, now in his thirties, didn't set out to rent the attic of his childhood home during his childhood, but the rent was considerably cheaper in 197? and in the end he had no choice. This warp made nostalgia material, and suppressing his painful memories of childhood was an elusive epiphany to strive for, rather than a malaise to be worked out through psychotherapy.

johnny werd worked too damn much at the cream pie factory
that week and he started to get a little... weird. you know what i
mean... weird. "weird"? you get it don't you? just a fraction weird.
anywa

jonnny, weird, camehome lateatnight after having willfully
established his absenteeism his refugeeism ifyouwill (i won't)
asitwere (it wasn't). he blewoff the jr.highschoolopenhouse in
favor of a night at home completely weary after working filling
pies... sitting. sittin. sitt. what a bastard! anyho

j.werd just then decided to become a fascist. it was much easier
he reasoned then being socialist or some other such "humane"
alternative political system. listen to johnny now, he's not become
a parrot for the marxistsloganranters railing on the Werd Jr.
Community College Campus. what a shithead! what a wretch!
fascism is much easier he reasoned because you pick one or three
or five rules for human behavior and figure out a polite way to
kill everyone who does not abide by them. that's much easier
than figuring out what everyone wants and how to work together
to achieve what everyone wants, i think. then he puked wretched
spew. Too many cigars. but he felt better afterwards and trailed
off to sleep, black phlegm trembling upon his snoring lip. what
a jackoff! what a jerk! what a dick! there he goes. fucking
everything all up. workaholic lemonjuicevitriumeyedwombatsuck
ing peninsula him. he coulda been a famous chemist but no.

anytim

sicker. listen. there he coughs, spewing all out into the night.
arresting spiral notebooks so his dreams can take flight.
and who cares about them? give it up, he lashed against the
fortress of his impotence his leeched bleached and impeached
badlifestyleasaurus, man. he's out of the running for the gold.
that's the breaks, Jake.

WELL? you shouldn't have, through inaction, caused that about which you are complaining, to happen.

then they would angrily stuff his fifty dollar bill in their wallet and tromp off to the parkinglot.

falling asleep that night John was filled with bliss. the werds "i wish i were dead" had been drifting through his cerebellum since the moment he terned thirteen. tonight he thought "i'm glad i'm dead. i'm glad i'm already dead." he doesn't have to werry about suicide anymore. suicide... Sue i side. nope. not a concern. the other members of the chemistry club were mad at him for being late to the meeting the day he hung himself. Angrily they phoned his home again and again. he hadn't tied the noose quite right and was hanging between the livingroom curtains reaching for the phone, which was on an endtable he couldn't quite reach. it rang seven times. his face was growing quite red. the phone rang seven times again and werd was just able, by pulling the curtains open using the curtain open pulling cord to swing by his neck just close enough to the phone to kick it onto the floor and screamed "HELLO?" but the guys at the chemistry club had already hung up so there was a click and a dialtone and a recorded message and an obnoxious beeping to indicate that the phone was off the hook. they wouldn't even have the good clean sense to throw him out of the club he fumed, slowly passing out. they would ridicule him in the hallways and... what could he do?

he couldn't attend in class because he was too exhausted from chemistrywork in the late hours. his teachers conspired. they had no interest in the sciences so why should he? they went to bed after a saucer of warm cream (curling purring arching their back against the ceiling and eventually coming to rest on enormous silk cushions) so why shouldn't werd? everyone else didn't do it so why did he? it couldn't possibly have been genetic. it must be learned. but who taught it to him. all the teachers, the chemistry teacher included, looked at one another suspiciously. who taught Werd chemistry? it couldn't have been one of us we never taught him anything

and they all went home to sleep on silk cushions.

after he awoke his head began to throb mightily. running his

fingertip along his greasy forehead furrows he could actually
feel veins bulging from the blood that could no longer flow freely
to his neck around which a rope was tied. he struggled with the
bind and accidentally put his foot through the plate glass window
leaving streaks of blood running down his thigh which spattered
the rug. finally, twisting, thrashing, he pulled the curtainrod
from its moorings and came crashing down on the endtable. after
a while he picked himself up from the debris of broken lamp
and stumbled across the room. the curtains trailed from the
curtainrod which hung from the rope still lashed about his neck.

i'm already dead, he murmured. as soon as he put the phone
back on the hook it rang. should I answer it? i'm dead.

i guess my friends will watch me fade into invisibility now

getting thinner and less substantial a toothpaste gaze upon

the cold minds flowing through the air. i am a pastel

skeleton. night will pass through me revealing my delicate

bone structure and coughing will become severe and difficult

to hear as i am costly air. articulate and silent ossifying

into nonexistence. i was a lost cause. now i am on pause.

johnny werd mumbles into microphone producing only feedback.

evaporating sublimating flesh fades. dissipating dissolving

overexposed and ghostlike werd is mumbling in the breeze.

& this important foreshadowing was ruined by this selfreflexive parenthetical footnote's admission of intent)
% *Webster's Ninth New College Dictionary.* 1983. Merriam-Webster: Springfield, Massachusetts.
\* he is fredflinstone: Igor Stravinsky wears horns on his left shoulder. Carl Stalling wears wings and a halo on his right.
~(sicnifigant)
^in a lobsta joint in caype cawd
\* (not LED) fight the war on acronyms (not the WOA)
$I just gobbled the last mouthful of muscle relaxant and will soon boil away in a liquid smear. Syringes wilt, this stuff is STRONG. Baby... Well, any last words..? The paragraph you just read utilized a POV transfer by *vision*-this is very important-in a Hagy sequence fashion style. This important writing technique was developed at the Yert conference in Brazil. The main issue at the Yert conference was a program to truncate lowercase letters in order to fit twice as many of them on a page. This posed a few dillemmi: namely, t and f became r among other things I am too drunk too figure out. Drunk with relaxant my fingers now thinning in consistency. the typing is pounding them into stumps, all three knuckles compacted... Naturally, as can be expected, of course, as is usual in these matters, which is par for the course... both of us drunk, me with the lastfistful of musclerelaxant, Werd with aesthetic outrage, his ruined concept. he was riding his bike back to his secret laboratoy on--now i forget what the name of the street is, but it runs just south of urbana high, you take that--to continue work on his anticommunicator---a strange device that would scramble matter----the basic building blocks on the level of electrons protons and--and you go east, take a left on anderson--neutrons----into Brunian configurations---i mean if you looked at the results under an electron microscope it would look just like one of Herbert's graphics--which is just after vine--so Werd dragged his bicycle into the gigantic aircraft hanger and snapped on the lights--and it'll be on the right. I continued walking home, putting my best foot forwards to take the first step of the journey of ten thousand kilometers. is that a decakilokilometer or what i mean give me a break, give me something i can latch on to like miles, miles make sense. i mean how many feet are in a mile. look here--how many? wait, say it slowly...

Give me some text with silences in it.